# A TALE OF ?6

# George Morris De'Ath

## CHAPTER ONE

All things must begin somewhere, and all things must end somewhere. And, in truth, most stories, sooner or later, are about blood.

Dark days were ahead. It could be smelt in the stained air, tasted in the poisoned waters, felt in the dying earth, and seen in the raging flames. Much would be destroyed and many would suffer, there was no denying that, yet none would stand to face the growing darkness that lurked and conspired in the shadows, ready to strike like a viper when the time was right. Hiding in plain sight, the signs all there, it was obvious, if you knew where to look that is...

Turbulent winds blew, rattling the spiked branches that jutted outward in the dark forest. Thick clouds hung overhead, threatening a storm in the distance with the faintest of rumbles. Something wicked was brewing on the horizon. A way ahead was clear, though, in these parts, wrong turns were easy to make. Some roads would even appear to loop back on themselves like a hanging noose. It was easy for a stranger to get lost.

Puddles of autumn rainwater filled the deep potholes that scared the tarmacked road, thanks to the winter storms and other miscellaneous agitators that had torn up the road like open wounds. Yet the trail still led relentlessly to its isolated path ahead. Black and still, the shallow pools in the gravel skin appeared more like blood in the glow of the moonlight. Ripples suddenly began to form as the ground began to bombinate with a certain vibration of speed and force. It was a car, an old vehicle, pumping through the dark woods. Searchlights illuminated the way ahead in the dense mist as the roar of the engine awoke a murder of cawing crows that began to follow above. A winning grin cracked across a youthful face. The face of a beautiful, young man, to be exact. He had strawberry blonde, short locks and striking blue eyes that shone out from behind a pair of square glasses, alive with positivity at what the night may offer him. He was well built, with a muscular, toned physique beneath a white shirt. Meticulous fingers tapped along to a cheery beat on the radio: 'Always Something There To Remind Me'.

Trees encroached overhead as he passed, like claws ensnaring prey, snuffing out the brief glimmers of sapphire light above. The boy manoeuvred around the buckled trenches in the road with glee ridden ease as his reserved hums grew to bellowing vocals. *Life is good*, he thought. *This is good.*

Suddenly, without warning, a body sprung out ahead. The young driver swerved and slammed the brakes on his car, causing his tyres to screech as if in pain. His fingers dug deep into the stirring wheel of the car as his lungs inflated with both shock and adrenaline. Panting, he checked his rear view mirror to see…nothing. Turning to view every degree of sight he could, again, nothing. Curiosity was always his weakness. He was inquisitive and overconfident. Blowing out huffs of air, he grabbed a torch from the glove compartment, switching it on to show a sturdy beam. He kept the engine running and there was a click as the car door opened. His flat feet crept out and his neck jerked about, struggling to see sight of anything in the pitch black of the woods. Even with his spotlight, he could only make out a few bushes, shrubs and stumps.

"Hello? Is someone there?" he called out. "Hello?" Snap! Something ahead moved. Cautiously moving into the beams of his car, the torch revealed a broken branch. Was it thrown? Placed? Or was it just fallen debris? A sudden breeze drifted it away to the side. A shadow washed over the young man, and he turned to see a form of a body blocking one of his car lights. Blinded by the other bulb, he rose his hand, before noticing the figure appeared to be limping. "Hello? Are you okay?" he asked as his gaze adjusted to see a young woman, looking somewhat worse for wear. The girl's long, dark hair billowed like a dandelion head in the wind and her leather jacket sparkled. She was pretty, but looked desperate as she hobbled slightly toward him with heavy hooded eyes and thin, parched lips.

"Oh God!" The boy frowned.

The girl quivered as she attempted to waddle closer to him. "Please help me," she rasped.

"What's...what's happened to you? Are you hurt?" he asked, looking her up and down.

Seemingly out of breath, the distressed girl collapsed to her knees as the young man swiftly grabbed her in his arms in support before rising her up. "Oh, you poor thing," he said, winching her up, her arm around his shoulder. She hopped on one leg as he guided her towards his car. "Come with me," he said kindly, opening one of the back seat passenger doors. "My family cabin is just down the road! We can get you cleaned up and call someone, maybe a doctor in the morning, if you need one."

The girl swallowed as she locked a sincere gaze with her saviour. "Okay," she said, nodding and settling into her seat, as the sweet stranger clasped his seat belt on and began to drive them safely ahead to sanctuary. Unbeknown to the boy, a cunning smile crept across the girl's face.

*Twenty minutes later...*

Jets of hot water cascaded over the young woman's body. A shower was just what she needed, relaxing her muscles for what was to come. It also gave her an opportunity to clean up the wound on her knee she had gifted herself. As she rinsed her face, through half closed eyelids, she could still visualise the outside of the cabin she currently found herself in. Rustic, off the beaten track, isolated, complete with a creaking door and floorboards. It was like something out of a horror movie, but she liked it.

She recalled that the vegetation all round was dead and withered, as if all life had been sucked out of it, demonstrated by the endless expanse of twisted, dry vines and tortured trees. It was as if the whole place had been corrupted by an invisible poison that had soaked into the roots in the ground. It was a treacherous environment, where it would be easy for someone to fall or hurt themselves. *Full of ways to die*, she thought grinning. And amongst the strangling thorns and decay of the murky woods, lying in wait, was this unsuspecting cabin.

Sneaking a peak, briefly, as she opened her eyes once more below the shower stream, she swore she could see a shadow watching her through the shower curtain. Springing to action, her wet hand pulled back the Bates Motel nylon to reveal…nothing. *Must just be a trick of the mind*, she concluded.

Turning the fountains of healing waters off, she stepped out on to a fuzzy matt. Covering herself with a towel, she demisted the mirror with a swipe of her hand. She could now see herself, wet and naked. How did she end up here? Well, she knew that, but still. This was never the plan, not in life anyway. But it was what it was. No need to think about it now. She hadn't chosen this life, she figured, it had picked her.

Looking down she saw a collection of colourful clothes. Colour was never her usual fashion choice. Black was more to her taste; simple, slimming and usually stylish. These clothes were too much. As if a lion had eaten a parrot and then vomited them out. Yes, colourful vomit was what sprung to mind as she picked gingerly through them.

Wincing as she knelt down, she bit back the pain she had inflicted upon her knee. She had to appear to be sincere, and rejecting this guy's sister's charity dumpster pile of clothes was no way to go about that. There was no alternative; she would have to choose something from the disastrous selection of clothes and get on with it.

Moments later, the wounded hitchhiker managed to limp through to the main body of the cabin, her hair still dripping. She looked around. The lounge area was a cosy room with two squashy armchairs set before a raging fireplace, and a battered leather settee. Two antler chandeliers hung from the ceiling, casting spiky, thorn-like shadows around the room. The fire was glowing warmly, the flames that dancing in the grate. The walls were made up of solid logs and held an array of different animal heads that appeared to watch her. Decanters of differing liquors sat on a side table. Ornaments and family photos were dotted around the room. She peered at one of the photographs; a mother, father, daughter and three sons. The guy who picked her up being the oldest son, it seemed. All happy and normal. As she made a note of her surroundings, the young man entered holding a tray containing two cups, a sugar bowl, milk, biscuits and a steaming pot of tea. He was easy to look at, with those golden lion locks, dazzling sapphire eyes and perfect bone structure. But she wouldn't let his pleasant looks distract her, not even slightly.

The young male halted momentarily and peered through his spectacles to see his guest wearing a purple T-shirt with a yellow smiley face accompanied by some jeans and fluffy slippers. He chuckled. "Oh, I see my sister's clothes fit you." He paused, lifting his gaze. "Nicely even." He placed the tray down on a table that sat between two chairs beside the fireplace. A silent awkwardness filled the room as the pair stood staring at each other. The young man smiled. "I made you some tea?" He gestured to the tray and then indicated to the chair for her to take a seat.

A frown crossed the girl's face, as the boy licked his lips. "I found some hob nobs in the cupboard. Hmm…do you like a hob nob?" he asked, wanting to build some level of trust, only to see the young girl's clearly confused face. People were never nice without a motive, especially young boys. Well, from her experience anyway.

"Won't you tell me your name? Or what happened?" The boy's hands clasped together in a saintly pose. "Did someone attack you?" he asked in apparent concern.

"No." She hesitated. "But something did, I don't know what?"

"Oh?"

The girl twitched slightly, before turning away, as if shy. She was meticulous with each expression, one wrong move could ruin the disguise that she had so carefully constructed over years of perfecting the tactful art of manipulation. "My name's Anna, Anna Jones," she answered, with a warm smile.

The boy's face lit up. "Oh well, it's nice to meet you, Anna, please sit." He motioned to the armchair beside her which she sank into with ease. "I'm Luke."

"Nice to meet you, Luke," she said, as he leant over to pour her tea, like an old-fashioned gentleman, and then his own. Her lips tugged themselves unwillingly into a smile.

"Here, a cup of tea. Get that down you and you'll soon feel better." He sprang up again. "Oh, where is my head! Milk or sugar?" he asked.

"Oh, it's fine," Anna answered, grasping her saucer as she reached over to plop one sugar into the cup and added her own milk. "I've got it." Stirring her hot tea with her spoon, she took note of Luke not adding any milk but instead adding an excessive degree of sugar cubes to his brew. She lost track of how many. It must have been at least five or six even. *He must like his tea black as night and sweet as sin*, she thought. Unexpected, but not unwelcome. As she blew away the steam, Anna took a blistering hot chug and whelped a little. Luke looked up with concern. It wasn't the heat, however, that took her by surprise.

"Needs more sugar," she gasped never having had tea like it. Strangely dry and yet sour? It was unlike anything she had tasted before. A part of her wondered if it was poison, Anna was paranoid like that. But no, they were both drinking from the same pot and, besides, this helpful son of a normal family wasn't the type. Luke chuckled a little as she followed his lead and grabbed four more cubes, dunking them in and mixing them before taking another swig to find the taste far more pleasurable than before.

"Like me, quite the sweet tooth I see," Luke teased, sipping from his cup. He then jumped a little in his chair and passed her a basket of blood red forbidden fruit. "Apple?" he offered.

Seeing her own reflection in the polished skin of the succulent bunch of red delicious, and then the pearly grin of Luke, Anna declined. "No, no thank you. I-I've never been a fan of red apples," she confessed.

"Suit yourself. More for me," he said, placing the basket back down to the floor. "I love red apples, so sweet." Luke's face scrunched slightly as he recalled the tantalising taste.

Anna sipped her drink. "I prefer green."

"Oh, bitter!" Luke mocked.

A silent pause fell between the two, followed by a sudden burst of joint laughter that soon settled back into quiet nothing.

"So tell me again, what was it that chased you in the woods?" Luke questioned.

Anna put down her saucer and sat upright as she began to caress her arm. Coming off as nervous in thought. "I don't know, it was something? Like a wolf, only not a wolf?" she whispered.

"Sounds spooky." Luke's pupils dilated as another silence filled the room. "You're not from around here, are you?" he said with intrigue.

Caught off guard for a second, Anna quickly brought her cup back up to her face. "No, how did you guess?"

"Just a feeling." Luke's fingers entwined as he leant in towards her. "Are you hurt at all?"

"No, I think I just scratched my knee when I fell over, that's all."

"Oh right…"

"You said this is your family's cabin?" Anna quickly changed the subject.

"That's right," Luke said, leaning back in his chair once more.

"And when are they coming back?" Anna asked, wanting to know how much time she had.

"Oh soonish I think, they went hiking earlier today. It's sort of a family vacation! "I had work," Luke stated. "Boring office job, before you ask."

"How many of you are there?" Anna replied. "Your family I mean."

"Let's see, there's my mum, my dad, my two brothers and my sister – whose clothes you're wearing right now." Luke grinned.

"Right!" Anna smiled, confirming the numbers that checked out with the photo she had seen earlier. She would have to make this quick, before they got back. No need to make this any messier than it needed to be. He was looking at her, what could she say? A cross hung above the fireplace. Bingo. "You're family's religious, I take it?"

Luke almost choked on his tea. "My parents are, me and my siblings not so much. But...you know."

Suddenly, Anna began coughing, rough and continuously.

"Oh dear, you're not gonna die on me, are you?" Luke joked.

"No!" she gasped, covering her mouth. "Sorry, do you have some water?" Her voice sounded scratchy as she continued hacking.

"Yes, of course." Luke jumped up and left the room. "I won't be a sec."

As Luke hastily ran out the room, Anna continued coughing up the performance of a lifetime. Making note of his footsteps in the next room and him grabbing a glass and running the tap, Anna began pocketing some expensive looking ornaments, which to her were now souvenirs. Quickly, she jumped back into her seat as Luke came in, passing her a glass of refreshing water.

"There you go," Luke said.

"Thank you," Anna managed to say, gulping the drink which enabled her to stop the forced coughing the second the water hit her lips. She sighed in fake relief. "Oh that's much better."

Luke exhaled. "Oh good. Had a frog in your throat?" he said, sitting back down to face her.

"Something like that."

Luke looked down at his twiddling thumbs. "What would you like to do? Would you like to eat? Stay the night? Get your bearings?" He raised his brow uncertainly. "Then we can get you home tomorrow morning?"

Anna's smile widened, as if she was touched by the notion. "Yes, yes please, that would be wonderful. And so kind."

"Not kind." Luke shrugged off the compliment. "You've obviously had a night of it. It's just the right thing to do." His chin rose high, repulsing Anna somewhat.

"Well, thank you anyway." Her cheeks lifted as she summoned up her best attempt at a grateful smile. The cross burnt the corner of her eye. "Sorry, you didn't get to finish what you were saying. Are you religious?" she asked once again.

"Oh, I wouldn't say I'm a hardcore Christian or anything like that." Luke confessed, looking into his cup. "I don't even know if I believe in God, I mean things just happen, what the heck, am I right?" He gulped his warm beverage.

Anna's eyes slit in evaluation, scrutinising him, thinking. He was attractive, but many men were. He was somewhat amusing from what she could tell, which was rare. And she suspected that he was more intelligent than he actually let on. At least on first impression anyway.

His head lifted to meet hers. "If God existed why would he allow all the horrible things that happen in the world?"

"Maybe God is dead?" Anna replied.

Luke gazed through his glasses, at his guest and grinned. "Ooh you're a dark one aren't you?" he said, giggling slightly.

"Not really, just matter of fact, everything has to die. Why not God?"

"Touchè." Luke pointed a finger. "Everything does have to die at some point but does that necessarily mean it's gone for good?"

"Sorry, I'm a little slow, what do you mean?" Anna asked.

Luke paused, enjoying the warmth of the fire beside them. "Do you like ghost stories, Anna?"

Caught off guard by the question, Anna floundered slightly. "Erm...sure! Who doesn't?"

Luke picked up his saucer and began stirring his tea with the spoon. "Well, how about a ghost story, you know, to pass the time, on this spooky night, while we're waiting for my family to get back."

Anna looked uncertain and Luke hesitated before continuing. "Here's one," he said. "It's classic, a ghost story with just a hint of...something else. It begins at a school named Hawkthorne Prep."

Tapping his spoon against the rim of his cup, the noise emulated the chime of a school bell, as if Luke was letting her know that class had just begun...

## THE FINAL LESSON

Shoes clicked along the clean paving stones that led to the tall gates of the prestigious and secretive all-girls school of Hawkthorne. Every brick had its place, every inch of grass was trimmed to perfection. Every step made was in unison. The girls waved and whispered as the school's newest student passed through the gates. Sarah, an ordinary girl, with ordinary gifts. It was strange how the students and staff seemed to blend into the place, as if a part of it. And there was Sarah, a newcomer, a stranger, sticking out like a bludgeoned thumb.

The architecture of the building borrowed from the purist of Gothic revival styles, though its structure was subtly medieval, with flamboyant elongated windows, tall stone pillars, and stone arches. Sarah soaked up the sights as she moved through to the main building itself.

Inside, the vibrant floors and walls were opulent, lavish and ornate. The whole place oozed femininity; the warm reds had an inviting feel, romantic even. It was a lush, but slightly decaying, little world, as illustrated by the peeling gold leaf flaking from the plasterwork on the ceiling above.

Sarah was now sitting in the dim office of Miss Willard, the school's headmistress; a mature woman with pronounced cheekbones. She simmered with radiant energy that twinkled out of her light blue eyes and complimented the swirling markings on her smart clothing, a blend of nocturnal purples and midnight blues.

Sarah found herself clasping her sweating palms, resisting the urge to stroke her hair, a tick of hers that she displayed when anxious. She was unwilling to show any form of tension in her body, and she repressed her inner sorrow and turbulence in front of the school matriarch. Instead, she set out to impress. She arched her spine, pulling back her thin, strong shoulders to present an unnatural sense of self-belief through her proud posture. Something the head was more than able to see through with her penetrative and perceptive gaze, though not unkindly it seemed.

"My heart weeps for you my dear, such a tragedy to lose both parents in that plane crash," the headmistress said. Her hand glided over Sarah's shoulder blades as she circled round the poor girl to reach her desk chair. "Truly, I am so sorry. Such a difficult thing to go through." Her senior, non-withered hands pushed forward a box of tissues.

Sarah couldn't hold it any longer; she let loose a tear, grabbing one of the tissues. "Thank you, Miss, sorry, what was it again?"

"Willard," answered the headmistress, lowering herself into her chair, her throne. "Wilhelmina Willard."

"Miss Willard. Sorry, I'm awful at names," Sarah confessed, blowing her nose. "Yes, it's been difficult for a while now. I think I've just needed…"

"Time?"

"Yes."

Miss Willard hummed in thought, interlocking her hands to reveal ruby-painted nails. "Yes, time tends to be the remedy for most wounds, doesn't it?"

Unsure whether to answer, Sarah stalled. "Yes?"

The headmistress's eyelashes flapped, like butterfly wings, before she spoke. "Your aunt tells me you wanted to come here to our very exclusive little boarding school for girls, for a fresh start?"

"Yes, and I also know your school is one of the oldest and most prestigious in the country. Coming here opens a lot of doors. I've heard you can get in or go anywhere if you went to school here."

A bashful hand flapped in front of Miss Willard's face. "Well, I don't like to brag but…yes."

Sarah nodded in acknowledgement, smiling through her tears.

Miss Willard smiled back, before rising up. "Come, let me show you around…"

As the minutes passed by, and Miss Willard showed Sarah around, she couldn't help get the feeling she was being watched. Whether it was the other students, the odd teachers or by something else, Sarah couldn't tell. It was as if something was lurking, hiding in wait. She just couldn't shake the feeling. It was like having something resting on your eyelid that you couldn't quite see. The uncertainty made Sarah shiver uneasily. Static energy pulsated through her skin, causing every hair on her body to stand on end. However, every reassuring touch from Miss Willard assured her she was safe, making her feel more bound to the place by the second. Willard's words were like velvet. Soft and luxurious. Empowering and comforting. For some strange reason, despite not knowing the woman for long, Sarah trusted her new headmistress, liked her, even.

      They strode down a foreboding hallway that seemed to come to life as foliage threw sinister shadows through the skylight above, reaching out as if to grab the poor girl.

      "Let me give you a brief history of the school, my dear. Hawkthorne was founded by Eleanor Hawkthorne back in the twelfth century. An institute for bright, inspiring young women, at a time when the world didn't believe females could, nor should, be doing such things. Learning, developing, reigning."

      Willard halted, stopping for them both to gaze about the evergreen courtyard they were now centred within. The courtyard was aflame with autumn colour, not just from dying leaves but prospering flower heads that spiralled upward, glowing in the hazy sunlight. Miss Willard inhaled and sighed. "This is a very special place, Sarah, for very special young women. I'm sure you will live up to our highest expectations…hopefully," she teased with a wink. She then turned her attention to two girls, watching from the side like vultures waiting to pounce. "Ah! Flora and Dora. Come."

      Willard crept behind the girls, who looked identical, inserting her head between them, like a mother. "These are some of your fellow classmates…twins. Say hello, girls."

      "Hello," the twins said in unison, without breaking eye contact.

      "This is Sarah, she will be joining us here. I want you both to make her feel welcome in her new home. Now, please show Sarah to her room. And be nice to her," she ordered.

"Oh we will." The twins grinned unnaturally.

"Good," Miss Willard said. "See you soon, Sarah, and do let me know if there is anything you need." Her arm rested once more on the girl's shoulder, sending what felt like a pulse of nurturing energy through her core, soothing her.

Sarah took a moment to compose herself, her head in a cloudy haze, before coming back to the present. "Will do, thank you, Miss Willard," she said, nodding politely.

"My pleasure. I have high hopes for you, Sarah," said the dark-haired woman as she began to make her exit. She had other matters to attend to. Pressing matters.

Sarah turned back to her supposed new friends. Both were grinning like Cheshire cats at her. "Hi, so which one is which?" she asked, in an attempt to stop the toothy display.

"I'm Flora," said the twin on the left.

"I'm Dora," said the twin on the right.

"We're sisters," said both twins in unison.

With everything that had happened lately in Sarah's life, these two were a quirky, yet unsettling, change; a distraction. Weird, and a little creepy, but harmless, surely, Sarah concluded. "Okay, cool," she replied, looking around to see they were the only ones around. "So where is everyone? It seems a bit dead for a school. Even a private one."

"Oh well, most of the girls take night classes," Flora stated.

Sarah frowned. "Night classes?"

"Yes," said Dora. "Regular classes occur during the day, extracurricular ones are taught at night."

"Okay, what sort of extra curriculum classes are there?" Sarah asked with interest. Her question was met by a dead response as the two mischievous girls side-eyed each other with a giggle.

"All sorts," they said together.

Nodding, Sarah attempted a smile.

"Here, let us show you to your room," Dora insisted, guiding Sarah by the arm out of the courtyard and into the main building.

"Oh yeah, sure," Sarah replied, unresisting.

"This way," Flora beckoned, taking her other arm as they guided her through the empty hallways that echoed with a thousand distant ancient memories that were stained into the walls.

Flora opened up a door, revealing a small room with an en suite bathroom. The ceiling was high up, with oppressive, pendant-shaped stalactites that hung down, reflecting a somewhat Tudor design influence. Very grand for a mere student, they made Sarah feel slightly claustrophobic as she entered the room to reveal more peeling plasterwork.

"Here you are, your own private room," Flora indicated, her twin by her side.

"Thanks," Sarah stated, dropping her bag on the floor with a thud.

Swinging her arms Dora said, "We're going to bed soon, we have to be up early tomorrow."

"Ah okay, think I'm going to have a bath anyway. I need to freshen up," Sarah replied. "I feel so grimy."

Flora paused in the doorway. "Lovely, we are the second door to the left if you need anything."

Taking a bouncy, springy seat on her new mattress, Sarah's face glistened gleefully. "Okay, thank you, Flora and Dora."

"No problem, Sarah," Dora said.

"No problem at all," Flora said, as they both lingered in the doorway.

"Goodnight then," Sarah said, waving them off.

"Goodnight. Sleep well," the pair remarked together.

Sarah shut the door, sealing her from the outside world. In that moment, she felt a wave of invigorating new possibilities sweep over her. This truly was a fresh start for her. An escape from it all. Rummaging through her bag, she got out her most prized possession. The only one she could not be without; a photo of her with her parents. As she looked down, she could recall their voices, kind and pure. They were good people. A single tear dropped on to the frame. Pulling herself together, Sarah placed the photo on her bedside table, caressing it gently with longing memory.

Soon enough Sarah had unpacked the small amount of things she owned in accordance to how she liked them to be placed around the room. After all, that was what her mother had taught her, a cluttered room was a cluttered mind, and that was the last thing Sarah needed right now. Her uniform was already laid out for her on the dresser, ready for tomorrow. Now all she needed was a bath, to cleanse herself of the past, or so she wished.

Foaming bubbles rose from the warm waters in her bathtub. Easing herself steadily into the tub with euphoric anticipation, the radio speakers played: 'Baby I'm-A Want You'. Calming and untangling the woes that had been swirling around in her head all day, Sarah shut her eyes. Allowing herself to be taken away from it all. She was unaware of the shadowy presence that quietly observed her naked young form from the corner of the bathroom. Suddenly, the radio began producing crude static to Sarah's dismay as she began tinkering with it.

"Oh come on," she complained, pressing buttons until the static turned to silence. The quiet was broken only by the steady drip, drip of the tap. Sarah continued to bash the radio in the hope of producing some kind of result, to no avail. She liked noise, it kept her from thinking. Distractions were always welcome in Sarah's world, no matter how small. Soon, giving up, the girl sighed and dropped her hands down in aggravation, hitting the cold and wet tiled floor. *How annoying*, she thought. Then something touched her left hand. Keeping calm, Sarah slowly crept over the top of the tub to look. It was a ball, a small red ball. Picking the toy up, she evaluated it. *How did that get there?* she wondered. She looked around. No clues or hints could be seen. Shrugging it off, Sarah threw the ball out into her darkened bedroom, as she sank back into the steamy tub, uncaringly.

Lowering her hand once more, she felt another touch. It was the ball hitting her, again. Gazing in the doorway there was nothing but heavy blackness blanketing her room. Sarah paused, curiously, before rolling the ball back into the darkness. Three, two, one…nothing. Nothing came back. It must have been a fluke. She leaned back in relief, but that relief died as she saw the ruby glow of the ball rolling back to her from the dank nothingness ahead. Sarah's lips grew as dry as a desert. Licking them she called out, "Is there someone there?"

Her question received no reply. Maybe the floor was just a bit wonky or uneven? Yes, it must be something like that. Rolling the ball back Sarah waited. This time, five, four, three, two, one…nothing? Rubbing her weary face, Sarah looked hard, awaiting the ball to make its return. Still, nothing. How odd.

Rising from her bath, Sarah slipped into her robe, cinching the belt tight around her waist as her warm, wet foot stepped down on to the bath mat. Grazing her toes on the furry friend below, she allowed them to dry. Sarah was not about to slip and die out of curiosity about a ball. Beginning to drain the tub, she pulled the plug, a gurgling noise began to rumble from the pipes. She was dry now. She could feel the flaky dead skin at her heel begin to peel off underfoot as she caught it on a corner of a floor tile. Sarah didn't care, she had find answers, as was her nature.

As she moved slowly and silently across the bathroom tiles, the bulb above flickered. Spinning around, Sarah felt a disorientating cloud descend over her. Once more, her hairs stood on end as she spun, feeling a pulsation, a connection to something or someone. Once again, out of sight, a figure lurked. Now clearer, however, a shadowy figure, decrepit and deathly looking, reached out to Sarah with a skeletal hand. "Sarah!" the spectre called out as the bulb burst.

Gasping for air, Sarah panicked, hobbling on her knees to reach her bedroom, turning the light on in there to reveal nothing. Stunned and paralysed with fear, Sarah took a moment as a feeling of rigor mortis took hold. Bringing herself to, she looked at her parents' photo. They wouldn't have wanted to see their daughter like this. This wasn't her. She was strong and brave. As Sarah grabbed her phone beside her bed, she felt a wave of brittle empowerment fuel her. It must be a prank, surely. Ghosts or whatever that was…weren't real. No.

Using the torch on her phone, Sarah paced slowly forward until she found herself at the bathroom's entrance. Inhaling and exhaling, she counted to ten and then jumped. Shining her torch everywhere she could spot nothing, nothing out of the ordinary. Nothing at all. She felt stupid now. It must have been paranoia creeping in or something, yes, something like that. Something like that. Shutting the door, Sarah decided to wait until morning to re-enter the room, when the morning sun could shine more light on the situation. Hopefully, she would feel better after some much needed rest. A clear mind would surely help put this whole thing into perspective. Unfortunately for Sarah, she would get little sleep that night, fearful that the horrible apparition would return…

Early the next morning, Sarah found herself distracted in both her first mathematics and English literature classes. What had actually happened last night? It wasn't her. *A prank*, she concluded. Yes, it made sense. She was the new girl at an elite boarding school. This must be part of some kind of initiation. Either way she didn't like it.

The first three hours passed slowly. Sarah now found herself marching through the hallways to her next class, history, until she spotted Miss Willard waltzing by. Sarah ran over to her. She would listen.

"Miss Willard!" she shouted, running to her, past all the other girls.

The headmistress stopped immediately and turned with a practised smile. "Ah, Sarah, I was meaning to speak to you. How were your first few lessons this morning?" she asked.

"Great!" Sarah's trusting eyes gleamed. "I really enjoyed them."

"Good to hear." Willard nodded, moving on only to be stopped once more.

"But…"

"But?" Miss Willard's chin lowered in question.

Sarah fiddled with the strap on her bag. "I…I think there was someone in my room last night?" she said cringing, not wanting to make a fuss.

The woman's strong jaw dropped. "Someone in your room? That is a very serious matter, Sarah. Are you sure?"

"I'm fairly certain." Sarah nodded, resisting the urge to tug on locks of her hair. "But I can't be sure. There was a little red ball rolling around by itself, my radio wouldn't work and someone seemed to be calling my name…"

The headmistress's brows arched in surprise, accompanied by an odd expression, as she attempted not to be patronising. Her eyes possessed that cold burn you got from holding ice too long. Her smile twitched this way and that, as though constantly changing its mind.

"Sarah, I don't mean to be insensitive but are you sure it wasn't the result of an overactive imagination?" She escorted her young pupil to one side. "I mean, it's understandable, you've been going through a lot lately. Might your mind be playing tricks on you?"

Sarah gulped her shame away, lowering her head. "Maybe, yeah. Probably, it's probably me just being stupid."

"Not stupid, my dear, cautious," Willard said, lifting the girl's chin up to meet her penetrative gaze. "Fear is a primal instinct, and when we think we're under threat we tend to over dramatise things that could merely be a breeze from under the door or an old radiator warming up."

An agreeing nod followed as Sarah lowered her lashes shyly. "Yes, it must have been something like that."

"Hmm…such a pretty little thing," Willard purred, softly caressing a loose strand of hair from Sarah's face. The intimate touch would be considered strange or inappropriate from most, but not Miss Willard, from her it was welcome reassurance. There was method in her approach. "Youth. Beauty. Is there anything more precious in this world?" she mused with a shade of regret before breaking away. "Oh well, you should get to your studies, dear."

"Yes," Sarah agreed.

"Run along now, little dove," Willard said as she watched over Hawkthorne's fresh meat. Something strange appeared to be afoot, but for now the wheels must turn and she continued on with her day.

Later on, in the late evening, Sarah yawned as she sat on her bed doing homework, a tiresome distraction, but a distraction nonetheless. Her ankles hung off the bed. She had settled into her new room quite happily, nested. A sudden buzzing came from her phone. It was her aunt, she answered.

"Hello, Aunt Sandra," Sarah said. "Yes, I'm okay, settling in. It's a lot of work; I've got so much homework to do." She awaited a response. "Yeah everyone's very nice, if not a little odd. Especially your friend, Miss Willard." She chuckled as her aunt responded. "Yeah, she's been really nice," Sarah replied. "Listen, can I phone you tomorrow? I'm really tired and have to be up early. Okay, love you, talk tomorrow. Yeah, bye."

Hanging up, Sarah decided it was time to sleep. Collecting and pushing her books and supplies into her bag she fluffed up her pillow and took a moment to gaze at her parents, captured in the frame, before turning off the lamp by her bed. That night, sleep came much easier but wouldn't last long.

Three am soon sprung round. A crack in the bathroom door widened, creaking more by the second. Then a thud hit the tiles, awakening Sarah. Through the blinds, the moonlight illuminated a prison bar pattern across the room. The door swung open abruptly, hitting the wall. Darkness, nothing but darkness. Sarah struggled to breathe, her chest felt tight as an uncompromising, tingling coldness took hold once again. The hair on her body pricking with anticipated horror. And then, the little red ball rolled about half a metre out. *Enough games,* she thought. "Hello? Who's there?"

A long silence took over the room and then a claw-like hand jutted out of the doorway, grasping the ball in its broken, dirt-ridden hands as they dug deep into the carpet, pulling it along to reveal a woman, or more like a corpse of a woman. She appeared as a mere husk, wearing a raiment that was chewed up and torn. Dark veining criss-cross patterns etched the wretch's ash white, peeling skin. Her dress that she dragged across the rough carpet had the look of seaweed about it, with lacy moist tendrils, though many other strips of fabric and bile were twisted and knotted. Skeletal, distorted, tortured, malformed and emaciated. A sinewy, grey-black smoky essence emanated from the ghostly form as its momentum and vigour grew. Sarah couldn't believe the shocking sight before her eyes and she shuddered in horror. Letting out painful screams, the female spectre dragged herself along the floor, reaching out to Sarah.

"Help! Someone! Please help!" shouted the terrified girl.

As the light was turned on, the drowned woman dissolved away. Sarah sat shaking, as Flora and Dora entered the room in their matching pyjamas.

"What's wrong?" Flora asked.

"We heard you scream," said Dora.

"Some…thing keeps coming into my room and creeping me out. It just dragged itself along the floor," Sarah said, still clutching tightly on to her covers as the two sisters looked at each other.

"Wait?" Flora frowned. "Did it look wet?"

"Yes, soaked." Sarah nodded, fighting back hysteria. "Drowned even."

"Oh. We may know what's going on," Dora said.

Sarah's neck jerked with a little pop. "Okay, so what's the big deal? What is that thing? Surely, not a ghost!" Her voice cracked as she spoke.

"Well…" Flora struggled.

"Oh, you've got to be kidding!" Sarah's eye's rolled, still unconvinced.

"What do you know about this place?" Dora asked. "It's origins."

"I know a woman called Hawkthorne built this school and yeah, that's it," Sarah said to their tense faces, sensing more. "Why is that not true?"

"It's the truth, just not the full truth," Flora replied, as the two twins now perched themselves on the bed beside her.

"What do you mean?" Sarah said, her toes curling up like springs.

Dora sighed. "Back when this place was being built Eleanor Hawkthorne was accused of witchcraft. The village people cut out her tongue and drowned her." The twin explained with disgust.

A flustered burst of heat broke out on Sarah's cheeks as she listened. "Christ."

"And it's said she still haunts this place." Flora's shoulders broadened. "A few girls have said they have seen things."

"Well, that's great but I didn't come to this school to be a part of an episode of *Scooby-Doo*!" Sarah exclaimed. "What can we do?"

"Do?"

"Yes, what can we do?" Sarah repeated, growing angry now. "To stop it? Get a priest? A psychic, see what she wants? I dunno? Hell, what about a Ouija board?"

"Never use a Ouija board!" the twins said together seriously.

Sarah was surprised by their sudden intensity. "What? Why?"

"Because it's the one thing our mother taught us," Dora said.

"Or rather, we listened to," Flora quickly added.

"But why?" said Sarah.

"Because you never know what you will bring forward," Dora answered.

"Damn!"

"No, instead we'll do a séance," Flora stated.

Sarah blinked, confused by the difference, but didn't question it. "Erm...okay then? How do you two know how to perform séances?"

The twins look at each other. "The internet."

Sarah paused in thought. "Fair enough. So how do we do it?"

Time passed. Sarah now found herself far below the prestigious school, walking through a maze of tunnels and crumbling staircases, in a secret cellar. It was a long, low underground room with rough stone walls and ceiling, from which round, ruby flickering lamps hung from chains. A fire was crackling under an elaborately carved mantelpiece ahead of them, and several ghastly painted portraits of previous headmistresses hung on the walls, watching. Rats scurried away into the cracks and crevasses hidden in the shadows. To Sarah, this cellar felt like a rotting womb. Like the belly of the beast of Hawkthorne. It was almost asphyxiating to the girl, she felt like an insect in a killing jar.

The twins were busily preparing, seemingly forming a pentagram symbol in chalk on the floor and lighting candles all around. Flora was reading from an old book they picked up from their room along the way.

"Okay, so how does this work?" Sarah asked, stopping herself from pulling her at her hair, as she looked surveyed her grim surroundings.

Rising up from the pages of the book, the twin stated, "We have to contact her and find out what she wants. Since you are the only one who has seen her, you have to stand in the centre." Flora pointed to the centre circle in the pentagram.

"Okay…" said Sarah, stepping into the circle, unsure what to do next. As she gazed around, she began to evaluate just how different this all was. It both worried and excited her. "I've got to say this looks a little…intense."

"It has to be. How else are we gonna get rid of your ghost problem?" said Dora.

Sarah shrugged. "I suppose."

"Just relax," Flora ordered her. "We're going to start."

Sarah breathed deeply. "Okay."

Flora and Dora clasped hands and closed their eyes. The twins began a chant that made Sarah, suddenly, feel a sense of great weight fall upon her feet. Locking her down, planted her to the floor.

"Done." Dora said as they completed the chant.

Panic kicked in as Sarah realised she couldn't move. She was stuck in the circle. "Wait, my legs." Nothing would work. "What have you done, I can't move!" she shouted in fear.

"Congratulations, girls, there's hope for you yet," said Miss Willard, revealing herself from the shadows along with a gaggle of other mysterious figures. The other students and teachers, dressed in their finest funeral vestments. They wore long flowing robes, heavy with embroidery and decayed finery, covered with sacrificial motifs and strange bone-like jewellery. It looked like ornately decorated armour.

"Thank you, Miss," the twins replied with a bow of their heads.

Sarah frowned in confused betrayal. "Miss Willard, what are they doing? What's going on? What is this?"

"The beginning my dear… and the end," the headmistress said, as she began to circle their prey.

Sarah's brain fried. "This…this isn't a school is it?" she questioned.

"Oh, it is." Willard nodded with certainty. "Like I said, for exceptional young women." Her heels clacked.

"What are you witches or something?" Sarah asked, feeling sweat dripping down her back.

"You could say that," the matriarch continued, unbothered by the term as she faced Sarah in the glow of the candlelight. "We have been waiting a long time for this moment, for you Sarah."

"Are you going to kill me?" Sarah's asked through quivering lips, unsure she wanted to know the answer.

"No, no. Not at all," the woman replied as if offended by the notion. "We are merely going to make you…greater. You see, we need a fresh, young new body for our...queen to embody and lead us through our despair. Our original queen." Her eyes lit up like a feline's.

"Eleanor Hawkthorne," Sarah murmured, realisation hitting her all at once. "The drowned witch, the one who has been watching me. Who I have been seeing."

"Yes. Oh, the wonders she will do in that young beautiful body of yours," she said ecstatically, viewing the girl as if she were merely an animal in a cage.

"But…my aunt will know, she will report I'm missing," Sarah said more confidently than she felt.

Willard's face remained impassive, then she began to cackle. "Oh, please, how naive can you be?"

A heavy, sinking feeling dragged Sarah's heart down, like an anchor as she realised the truth. "She's in on it, isn't she," she whimpered.

"Indeed. Who else do you think cursed your parents' flight!" Willard revealed proudly and without mercy.

Sarah felt as if she ceased to exist in that moment. It all came together in one distressingly dark moment, wrapped in nothing but misery and death.

"Why?" Sarah said, feeling both heartbroken and vengeful.

"Well, for you Sarah." Willard's pitch heightened as she leant in closer. "You were chosen. You were selected by our queen. Chosen for who you are." She grinned at Sarah maliciously.

Teardrops fell down the girl's cheeks. "All this…for me?"

"It was prophesied. Think of it as a great honour," Willard explained, stepping back.

"What, to die?" Sarah snapped.

"It's not death, more like taking a back seat in your own skin." Willard said theatrically.

A hiss escaped Sarah's lips. "No. This isn't real. This is just a dream."

Willard seemed amused by the girl's denial. "Believe whatever will settle your nerves."

"Please don't do this!"

"Sacrifices must be made," Willard insisted. "Dark days are ahead, the apocalypse is coming. Eleanor Hawkthorne will rise again, as will her master, our master. And by our queen's side, he will allow us to reign and lead and survive as his obedient subjects."

Sarah tried to force her legs to move, to pull herself out of the. "No, you can't do this!"

The headmistress leant in again and coldly repeated herself, "Sacrifices must be made."

Sarah tried to think through her fears, desperate trying to find a way out. "I thought you said I was going to be something great, so teach me," she said.

"Teach you? You're a meddlesome girl, nothing else. Cursed with more ambition than talent," Willard scolded. "Hawkthorne is one of the most powerful beings of existence and you get to restore her. Isn't that beautiful?"

Sarah's head shook as she began to cry openly, turning to the assembled cloaked figures, to Flora and Dora who stood to the side. "No. Please don't do this."

"Let the ritual begin," Willard commanded as the cloaked figures joined in a circle around Sarah, snuffing out her cries for mercy with their chants. Sarah struggled like a fish on land, but it was no use.

"Rise up, goddess, feel our flame," Willard screamed, as everyone else recited the serenade of death and rebirth.

"Rise! Rise! Rise!"

The room began to spin. Sarah's muscles seized up. She felt the cold breath of her admirer as she placed a crooked set of wet fingers on her shoulder. Their spirits and minds mingling now, though not naturally. Like oil and water. It felt like a glitch to Sarah, a computer virus taking hold. She did all she could to mentally fight back. Bursts of lights and colours popped, crackled and fizzed. Sparks flew in the mindscape of Sarah as the coven of students and teachers and Willard began to crumble with the sheer might of power on display. It was too much. As another cold, dead hand lifted, Hawkthorne let out a banshee scream, using one dripping, skeletal hand to tug hard at the girl's hair and another to cover Sarah's mouth and muffle her cries. Sarah contorted with pain and anguish before everything went black.

Alive, Sarah's eyes opened. Awake. She rose, feeling her body. All around her were dead bodies. The twins' corpses were curled up together in joint horror and Willard's back arched and contorted so much that it looked as if it could snap with just the gentlest of breezes. Sarah smirked, victorious as she rose up, now able to move and leave the circle.

She walked over to the mirror and gazed at the reflection presented. She grinned, gazing up and down the body, before saying to herself, "Yes, this will work, this will work nicely…"

## CHAPTER TWO

"That wasn't very scary," Anna said sarcastically in disappointment. She was opening herself up more now, still sat in the homely log cabin.

Luke frowned at the shun, biting on a biscuit treat that apparently went undeserved.

"Really?" he murmured, covering his mouth as he both crunched and spoke.

"No!" said Anna. "Ghosts and witches, body swapping? None of that stuff is real."

"How do you know?"

"Because it's not."

A flicker of a grin crossed Luke's face. "Hmm…I wouldn't be so certain," he teased, further aggravating Anna. She didn't like to be patronised, even though that wasn't the young man's intention. He stood tall, smoothing down his shirt as he moved over to present an African-looking fetish doll, sat as an ornament on a bookcase on full display. Luke pointed a slender finger towards the doll. "See this little bugger, he's caused more death and misery than anything you could find in these haunted woods." Luke sounded almost proud, as if he had carved the doll himself.

"That?" Anna rose in question. "What's so special about that doll thing?"

"It's cursed. Oooh!" Luke mocked, before adopting a more serious note. "This is a hoodoo tribal statue, blessed by the shamans of Haiti. Somehow it made it over to our waters. It grants wishes. Three wishes to be exact." His held up three fingers for emphasis.

Anna laughed. "Cool!"

"No, not cool." Luke frowned, standing between herself and the doll. "Every person who has made a wish on this…thing has wound up dead, or worse."

Anna's brow rose. "Really?"

"Yes, it is said one man wished to be rich, and what happened? He won the lottery, the next day he spent his money on a cruise."

"That's nice."

"The ship sunk," Luke added. "A lady wished she could lose weight, what happened? She was diagnosed with cancer. Another man wished to have his wife brought back from the dead only for her to come back, brain dead or something. He had to shoot her in the head out of mercy."

"Oh. I'm starting to see a theme here."

"Another man wished to live forever," Luke said as he began pace the room.

"What happened to him?" Anna queried.

Luke paused. "Actually I don't know what happened to that one, but probably something horrible like the others."

"That is if you believe in those sorts of things that is."

"Yes…"

Suddenly, Anna went to grab the statue like a naughty child in class. Quick as anything, Luke sprung forward, stopping her hand from connecting with the artefact. She fell on top of his surprising large and muscular chest. His heart was beating strong and hard, throbbing with masculine energy.

"Can I make a wish?" Anna asked, looking up to his glasses as she removed her soft hand removed from him.

"L-lord no!" Luke stuttered, back up. "Don't meddle with fate, let things play out the way they are meant to." He adjusted his spectacles which had been knocked in the commotion.

Anna rolled her eyes. "Oh come on now, do you really believe all that voodoo hoodoo crap?"

She got up and walked across the room. Luke noticed that she was no longer limping, at least not to the extent she had been earlier.

"I must say you seem to have perked up?" he said.

"Yeah, sure." She paused, before adding, "Ghost stories tend to do that to a person."

"Right…well, all the best stories have a bit of magic to them." Luke said with open hands as he sat bashfully, gazing at her. "Don't you think?"

"I can beat that story." Anna said bluntly, her competitive streak shining through.

"I'm sorry?"

"I can beat that, the ghost witch story," Anna stated, as if it were a challenge. She sat down opposite him.

He smirked, as he sat back, interlocking his fingers into his groin, ready for whatever would follow. "I'm all ears."

"In fact, the whole bringing someone back from the dead thing got me remembering one story in particular. And best of all, it's a love story…"

## AFTERBIRTH

'Spring blooms love in the most unlikely of places' read an advertisement, on a high city billboard, for a dolled up dating app. Past it strode a tall, self-entitled young woman with a strong chin, and a stocky, broad young man who found themselves walking along the same road at opposite ends, both looking down and texting on their phones. They did not appreciate the new life and beauty around them, they were so transfixed by the screen in their hands, their escape from the real world, something they both felt they needed as they had no one to share the real world with.

A collision course was set and primed as the sun shone down on the pair. Stumbling into each other, they dropped their phones and gasped looking to each other in surprise. The young man apologised and the woman grunted before he passed her phone up revealing his face. Their eyes met and connected in sync as the world around shimmered, seemingly giving off endorphin inducing attraction. Sharing a warm smile they exchanged names, Paul and Donna, and the rest was history. Dates to picnics, bowling, golfing, dinners, lunches, walks in the park, they did it all throughout the seasons that seemed to melt away whenever they were in each other's company. Before long, within the year that marked their first spring encounter, Paul got down on one knee and asked the question, to which Donna replied with a simple, "Yes."

Wedding bells rang out the following summer as they kissed, showing the world their shared love of one another. Months moved on and they bought an adorable little house together. Moving in was tedious but, together, they managed to make any task seem fun.

Before long, Donna craved a child to complete their perfect family. This was not as straightforward as she hoped and, after months of trying, the couple found themselves in a doctor's surgery being told of their slim chances at achieving her dream.

Donna came from a family of money, and she was used to getting her way. Paul blamed her for being born to a life of privilege, something he knew nothing of, but admired her efforts to overcome her inherent over-appreciation of the value of money and loved her for it. But this was something Donna knew she couldn't throw money at. What they needed was luck, and with time that luck came.

The spring fertility hit and a baby bump appeared. Nine months later, in the cold winter months, Donna found herself in hospital, in labour, until she wasn't any more. Their baby was born; Reggie. The perfect baby, with large sapphire eyes framed by fluttering thick lashes, accompanied by a head of blonde hair, Reggie had a winning laugh and grin-inducing smile. Their perfect family was complete. They were complete, fulfilled.

One month later, they were manoeuvring the pram, holding their precious prince, along the pavement on a busy street. The winds were blowing hard that day, as the couple shared a passionate kiss, taking a moment to appreciate and give thanks for their new life. For the briefest of moments, Donna let go of the pram and, with that, the coarse cruelty of nature took hold and blew its air, pushing the pram out into the busy road, just as a truck rolled by. The driver blared the horn and slammed on the brakes. Donna howled, a mother's cry, but alas it was too late. The child was dead, their child, Reggie, was dead.

Piercing white light stung the sight of the distraught mother and she shook in distress. Paul cradled his scared, sobbing wife in the hospital. "I can't believe we let this happen," she cried.

"It's okay, hunny." Paul kissed the top of her head. "We will get through this. I promise. It's okay," he soothed.

Donna sprung up in distraught anger. "No, it's not 'okay'," she yelled. "Our only child, most likely the only child we will ever have, is dead. And it's because we were stupid idiots!" Her voice broke off as she collapsed to the floor.

Paul knelt over his wife, taking her hands gently in his. "We can try again."

"Can we?" she said hoarsely. "It was luck that gave us Reggie. What's going to do it this time?" Mascara stripes streaked down her cheeks as the bereaved mother closed in on her misery. The baby's father let go of her, rubbing his rugged, stubbly chin in thought. He stood up and leant against the wall for support, knowing he would not find it from his apparent lifelong sweetheart.

"I don't know what to say, I wish I did," Paul said in shame as Donna looked up at him. "I'm-I'm so sorry." With that, he left the room.

"Paul, wait!" Donna cried out, as he went, now bitterly alone in her grief and heartache. A waterfall of tears cascaded to the floor.

Black speckled patterns appeared before Donna's eyes and she found herself losing focus. Her thoughts were soon overshadowed by another's presence. Looking upward she could make out the shape of someone; a hospital cleaner. An old, funny looking man with a mop and a cap and a bizarre hunched over physique, the result of scoliosis. His toothy grin was accompanied by rough, hardworking hands that offered to help raise her up. Sniffing loudly, she gave him her hand, allowing the cleaner hospital to pull her up. Coming to her feet, she stood taller than this odd little fellow who now adjusted his cap. She didn't feel like conversing with anyone, but managed to say, "Thank you."

"You're more than welcome. I'm sorry to intrude but I couldn't help but over hear your conversation. Terrible news, I'm so sorry. It's a tragedy. My heart feels for you, it really does. Would you care for a mint?" he said in a gruff voice, offering her an open packet.

Mints were the last thing Donna needed right now. She appreciated the kind offer, but didn't show it in her reaction. "Oh no, thank you, though that's very kind," she said, wiping away her tears with one hand, and reaching for her clutch bag on a nearby chair with the other.

"Suit yourself, anyway let me get to the point," the cleaner said, popping a small minty treat between his decaying gums and sucking on it loudly. "I know someone who may be able to help you with your predicament."

"Help me?" Donna's nostrils flared, somewhat insulted by the notion. "How can they help me? How can anyone help?" she hissed in his face.

"Oh well, I know a man who could do what you want, with your son, bring him back." He chewed his lip with relish. "Dr Barnum is his name."

"Ha!" Donna let out a sarcastic laugh. "Are you joking?"

"Do I look like I'm joking?" the cleaner said, as a long streak of drool escaped his jaw.

Donna paused in repulsion before continuing, "I've heard about him; the disgraced doctor and his lunatic experiments."

"Not at all, the man is a genius. A true artist. A visionary," the little old man said. "He just gets a bad rep. It would, at least, be worth a look into, don't you think?" His keys jingled as he leant in closer.

Her glare met crooked eyes. Donna was in no state for this cretin. "I'm not in the mood to be making deals with charlatans today, thank you," she insisted, beginning to make her exit, her heels clacking halfway out of the door.

Hobbling after the woman, the cleaner approached and whispered in her ear, "But he can give you what you want," he murmured. "No one would have to know, no one would tell, it would be your affair." His crooked grin cracked. "The good doctor can do what no one else can. It could be your one chance at getting your son back." His rank breath wafted in front of Donna. She hesitated momentarily, unsure, before turning to the cleaner.

"Take me to him," she said, through her tightly clenched jaw.

And with that, the cleaner's toothless smile grew.

Later, as the night passed, Donna found herself following the slow-paced cleaner along a serpentine-like path. She was carrying the bloodied remains of their baby son in a box, Paul by her side. A storm bellowed high above.

"Don, what the hell are we doing?" Paul said. "This doctor is a mad man; you remember the news reports about him a few years ago? We can't do this!"

Donna huffed, frustrated with her husband's overly cautious nature and unwillingness to take a risk. It was a quality she both loved and hated about him. "I'm willing to hear him out, it's the least we can do," she said, hastening her steps to move away from her husband. Paul was too quick for her and grabbed his wife by the shoulders, turning her to face him.

"Hunny, Reggie is dead. Dead is dead. It's very sad, I know, but let him rest," he said, pleading her to see past the madness of what they were doing.

"No, we are his parents!" Donna snapped. "He died because of us. It's our job to protect him, to do what's best for him. That's what I'm doing." Paul's face dropped. "Help me, help me to help our son," Donna begged. "Please. If there's even a chance we have to try."

Paul nodded in uncertain agreement. "Fine, but please don't just say yes to anything. I don't trust him or his lackey," he said, directing his comment to their guide, just ahead of them along the path, who turned and smiled.

"Ah, we're here. In ya get," the cleaner said, opening the doors to the old barn. Donna and Paul entered to reveal a mismatch of technology and filth. The floor was ridden with mud, wire cords and hay. Electrical equipment buzzed and sparked. Torn up blueprints and jars of strange, pickled, sewn-together animals covered every shelf and table top. The doctor stood with his back to them, tinkering with his rusty tools.

"Hello, old friend, I have brought you visitors." The cleaner coughed and bowed slightly, making his stooped back more pronounced. "And they have a favour to ask."

"A favour, I'm not in the business of favours," Doctor Barnum said, spinning round. He wore green goggles and a bloodstained uniform and was holding a ridiculously large saw and scalpel. Lightning flashed and thunder roared.

Paul froze at the stupidity of it all. "I'm already over this, come on, hunny, let's go," he insisted, tugging on Donna's arm. She pulled away from him, and moved towards the doctor, cradling her baby boy's remains.

"Answer me one thing, doctor," she said, scared of the answer she would receive. "Can you bring back the dead?"

"Donna!" Paul snapped from behind as the thunder cracked again.

"Reanimation?" he questioned with a serious tone. "Yes, it is possible. Granted it's only worked on a few occasions but it is possible." The doctor then turned towards to his discarded jars of monstrosities.

"Donna!" Paul said more urgently.

"Tell me honestly, doctor, could you bring back our son?" Donna asked, with hope.

"Maybe I could." He nodded, continuing to ponder as he moved away to his tools, thinking. "What is the child's age?"

"He was one month old," Donna said, caressing the moist cardboard.

Barnum's eyes enlarged through his goggles and he lifted them up in excitement to look at the mother. "A baby? I've never tried this on a baby before." He fizzed like a child on Christmas morning.

"Donna!" Paul rasped.

"Name your price," said the desperate mother.

The insane doctor sprung forward and touched the woman's cheek gently. Donna recoiled and pulled away. "My price is your smile."

"That's it?" she said. "So what is the catch?"

He gave an open hand signalled. "No catch, merely scientific intrigue." Barnum's demeanour lifted further. "My research could really benefit from such a case," he said pointing towards the box. "Is that the body?" Donna nodded. The cleaner pushed himself forward with his crooked spine and drooping jaw.

"Yes," he confirmed. "I managed to pick it up from the morgue when I was cleaning in there earlier."

Barnum gestured to have the box passed over, which Donna did. Paul clamped a hand on her shoulder from behind, and she gripped his resting hand. Biting on the thumb of her free hand, she watched as the bizarre scientist evaluated and made a verdict on the presented remains. He examined every inch with precision through his magnifying glass while the cleaner looked on, licking his ghoulish lips. Eventually, Barnum huffed in conclusion, shutting the box once again as he spun round, glee ridden.

"Oh, yes, yes, this will work very nicely," Barnum said.

Nails dug into Paul's skin as Donna squeezed his hand. She smiled, her emotions varying from grief and repressed self-anger to disbelief and hopeful surprise at the doctor's response. "When can you do it?" she asked.

"Tonight, if you truly desire it. The sooner the better."

"Tonight?" Donna gasped.

Paul, once again, grabbed Donna and took her to one side. "Donna, don't...."

"We have to Paul, for our son." She threw him off her, returning to the dastardly duo. "Do what you have to do. Just bring him back," she said.

"Very well. Leave me," said Barnum, clapping his hands together, feeling expansive suddenly. "I need to isolate myself in my work."

The cleaner grabbed Donna and Paul and began to pull them away, out of the barn, along with himself. "Come now, let the good doctor get to work on his sorcery," he said, shutting the barn doors behind them.

Inside the barn, surgical hands carefully began to play a crackling record, 'O Mio Babbino Caro'. On hearing this, Barnum felt cultured once more. It was a reminder of his past renowned life and his fingers worked in conjunction with the music, soothing his mind.

Barnum approached his operating table and tools. Synapses fired and flared as Barnum picked up the box, containing the dead baby, and lowered the specimen on to his operating table. He gazed at its mangled form wondering how he would replace the missing and damaged elements set before him, like a jig-saw puzzle. He liked a challenge. Pondering aloud, he reached for a rag beside him, dipped in a blend of hallucinogenic substance he had concocted, the key to all his 'best' ideas. Quickly, he breathed it in deeply for inspiration as his eyes shut, seeing a plethora of multi-coloured shapes and facets spring into his already sickeningly perturbed mind. Nothing! Many fascinating concepts but nothing that linked back to this particular project. And then, by merely opening his eyes, he had it; his pickled jars of stitched together animals.

Before long, he found himself hacking and stitching and sawing and sewing through the deathly pale, infant skin with his dirt-ridden, rust-covered tools, adding new elements to his toy. Repulsed by the rotting scent that trickled down the back of his throat he pulled on a mask and whipped out a magnifying glass to perfect his creation.

In little to no time at all, Barnum was finished with the reconstruction. Now all his marvellously unnatural being needed was a spritz of life, with some fresh blood and a jolt to the heart to get it pumping once more. He proceeded to inject the newly stitched together corpse and attach sharp clipping cables into the chest of the skin. It was time. He pulled down a large power switch, electrifying tendrils high above on tall aerials. Wires cracked, fizzled and sparked and he lowered his goggles to shade him from the engulfing heavenly light summoned through his scientific experiment. A megalomaniacal, ego-driven smile cracked across the mad scientist's face as the creature screamed a hellish roar and rose with its claws high, casting shadows across the walls of the barn.

Doctor Barnum rejoiced at his miraculous creation, his creature, yelling, "Alive, it's alive!"

Moments later, Donna and Paul hurried in, together with the rickety cleaner, as they saw the good doctor beginning to clean up his lab, his bloodied tools and clothes.

"You did it?" Donna asked in agitated joy and curiosity. "You brought him back?"

Barnum nodded. "Oh yes, he's over there?" He gestured to a covered cage.

Paul frowned in anger. "What, in that cage?"

"Oh yes." The doctor nodded. "He has a somewhat aggressive disposition. I'm sure he'll grow out of it. Take a look."

The doctor continued to tidy up as Donna and Paul slowly crept towards the blanketed cage. The smell was unbearable, an ungodly concoction of unnatural excretion and infestation. Lingering to lift the cover, Paul finally did it and unveiled their new son.

Both of the parents' faces turned to horror as they saw the monstrosity before them. Its pale, stitched together skin oozed out bile and blockages of inky rot. It was practically black blood that seeped out. It was covered in abnormal lumps and bumps and its beady, bright blue eyes contrasted its claws and impressive assembly of snarling teeth. As they drew closer, the monster pounced forward, beginning to growl and gnash its razor sharp piranha jaws in their direction. As Paul pulled back in fear, Donna smiled.

"Oh my God! What is that thing?" Paul questioned, insulted by its very existence.

"Our son, Paul," said Donna. She knelt down in the muck, eager to help her child entrapped in the cage.

"But…but it's not human!"

This didn't appear to concern Donna. "Oh no, he is, look at him," she said, grinning. "He still has my mother's eyes, look. He's just a little different that's all. But we can work with that can't we? He's still our little Reggie."

The growls began to desist as a maternal voice hummed, her cautious hand creeping through the steel bars to stroke a part of her child's head, soothing it somehow. "Oh look, I think he recognises me. Yes, Reggie, it's me, Mummy. I've missed you. I've missed you so much." Tears of joy fell down her face at the macabre reunion. She was ready to wake up from her dark dream, she knew this was real. "Oh I was wrong about you, doctor. You are a genius. How on earth did you do it?"

Her praise inflated Barnum's ego. "I used the needed organs and remains of other creatures," he replied.

"Amazing." Donna replied with a sigh, stroking the little tuffs of hair on her baby boy's head.

Barnum closed his medical case. "Truly remarkable, the human trial was a complete success."

"'Human trial?'" Paul repeated. "As in there haven't been any human trials before Reggie?"

"Well, no, only animal trials."

His fist clenched as Paul attempted to restrain his urges. "You left that bit out before didn't you?"

Barnum frowned and checked his pocket watch. "I didn't think it was relevant."

"Oh, marvellous work, doctor, truly marvellous work," said the cleaner.

The doctor received all the praise he could. He loved it, soaking it up like a sponge. "Thank you, thank you for sending these poor people to my doorstep, you have always been my favourite little helper," he said, tapping his accomplice on the head.

"Helper?" Paul said, stomping toward the pair. "This was your plan wasn't it?"

"Not at all, you needed help." The cleaner cowered away. "I knew Doctor Barnum could offer it."

"Oh pipe down, Paul!" Donna ordered. "Look at him. Look at our son."

Paul regarded his clearly delusional wife sadly. "Donna, that thing is not our son."

The father clamped his lips shut as he was met with a murderous glint of protective fury that swiftly took hold of Donna. She turned and growled at him, "Well then, I suppose he's still my son!"

Barnum placed a careful cough as to signal the time and, hopefully, break up their spat. Donna jumped up and, in a much kinder and grateful tone, said, "Thank you, for your services, doctor." She covered the cage, once more, and picked it up by the handle with careful ease. Then she exited the barn with a new lightness in her step as she muttered away to her baby Reggie.

Paul turned to look at the cleaner and Doctor Barnum, who were waving him goodbye as he turned to scowl at them. Like most experiments gone wrong, he did not quite know how this would play out next.

Some weeks later, Paul found himself adjusting to his new family life. He sat on his sofa, reading a newspaper, with the abnormal shrieks and screams of his fast-growing undead child piercing his eardrums. Trying to keep it together, Paul clenched his newspaper. The last thing Donna and Paul needed was yet another fight but he couldn't take this any longer. He felt like his ears were leaking hot with blood.

Paul rubbed his eyes and gave a longsuffering sigh. "Ah, for God's sake, shut that thing up!" he said angrily. His words bursting out like a damn that had been holding its waters for far too long.

Suddenly, the crying stopped. Donna entered the room, shutting the door behind her. She was sweating and trying to button up her bloodied, claw-marked chest. Paul looked at her, dropping his paper to the ground, and rushed to her aid.

"Donna? What's happened? Are you okay?" he asked, ready to rush her to the hospital.

"Oh it's just Reggie." She waved off the incident, as if he were just a scamp. "I thought he was hungry and I tried to nurse him, but I don't think it was milk he was craving."

Paul could see that. That open wounds on his wife's chest showed that much. That thing in there wanted blood. He could see the teeth marks even now as Donna tried to hide them beneath her shirt. He had tried to guzzle her dry. Like a leach.

"Donna, listen to me," he said. "That thing is not our son." The mother wriggled away from him, cursing. "It's not human!" Paul shouted over the cries that rose, once more, from the nursery.

"I will not listen to this again…"

"Donna please…"

"I will not hear it."

A sudden bang, accompanied by roaring whelps, came from the nursery. Instinctively, Donna sprung to her son's aid and ran in to find the crib knocked over. His holding pen.

"What is it?" Paul asked, entering behind her and freezing in horror.

Without thought, Donna began piling through the bundle of soft, shredded-up cuddly toys they had bought the creature, hoping to find him hiding in there, playing. "He's got to be in here," she told herself, as Paul watched. "Well, help me to look for him then," she said.

Stepping around his wife, Paul began to look under all the cabinets to see if the creature was hiding under them or in any other spaces it could fit itself into.

"Where could it have gone?" Paul said.

"Where could 'he' have gone," Donna corrected him.

They then heard a scuttle in the hallway. They quickly followed to see a trail of blood that led to the cellar.

Paul flicked on the light switch to no avail. "Damn." The light never worked down in the cellar, Paul had been meaning to fix it. He never imagined this kind of situation would arise, otherwise he would have made sure the light worked. He breathed heavily, beginning his journey down into the dark using the torch on his phone to light the way, Donna close behind.

"Stay here," he ordered Donna.

"But he needs me," she whimpered.

"Stay here," he repeated, his temper snapping. He felt the rickety stairs creak upon his descent down into the dark as the blood trail went cold. Moving the torch on his phone around, he could see an endless maze of towering boxes. The light triggered movement, noises from all around. Clambering and growls. Paul's heart felt like it beating out of his chest, and his veins seeping out of his skin as he prepared to face the child monster. He could retreat, leave this place, hell, burn it down, but that wasn't Paul. He was a man of principle, he wasn't ashamed to be scared, but he would rather die a man than a coward. He would do right by his wife, no matter what that entailed.

He spun round on hearing a mop fall. Paul jumped as he came face to face with a vampire decoration. His chest rattled, he brought himself too.

"Ah God!" he breathed.

"What is it?" Donna called down.

"Nothing, don't worry."

Then he heard another noise, coming from a corner. A sucking, gurgling kind of noise. Paul approached, cautiously, shining his spotlight on the back of the deformed child who was covered in blood and eating a rat. "What the hell?"

Without warning, the child hissed and leapt towards Paul who dropped his phone and screamed in the dark, scrambling and fighting to stay alive…

Later that night, Paul and Donna sat together eating dinner in silence. Donna's chest was bandaged up and Paul's arms were also bandaged as Reggie rested up in his newly reinforced crib that sat beside the table for them both to keep an eye on him. He was out like a light, fighting with his apparent father in the cellar had clearly exhausted him. Donna chewed on her pasta, not quite sure what to say to help with Paul's mood which she could tell was simmering more and more by the second. She sipped her wine before she began.

"Look, he was just a bit hungry, all kids get like it," she said. Paul dropped his cutlery and slapped his forehead with his palm. "We can work on it with him. Sure he's a little strange but what child isn't?"

Paul lurched over the table aggressively. "Strange! Strange? That is not 'strange' that is an abomination of nature, Donna! That thing is a monster!" He pointed to the crib. "When will you get it? That is not Reggie."

"How can you say that?" Donna stood, hand on her belly. "How can you be so selfish? We have been given a rare gift, we should appreciate what we have."

Paul huffed, exhausted. "That's the thing, Donna, I was happy with just you. You were enough for me. I never wanted kids, did I? But I knew you wanted a baby, even with your…condition." His voice quivered with emotion as his wife's eyes begin to water. "I tried and tried. For you. Always for you. But it was never enough was it, and it never will be. And lately I've realised that I'm the only one that can stop this madness, so I will." He sat back to continue eating his dinner.

Donna's broken expression turned to an abrupt laugh. She raised her glass, feeling strangely relaxed. "Oh please, what are you going to do?" she teased, wiping her tears as she took another sip of wine. "You're all bluster and no follow through. You won't do anything."

"I already have," Paul admitted as Donna struggled to move her weary limbs and keep herself awake. She felt strange and dizzy all of a sudden. She looked up to his uncompromising demeanour across the dinner table. "I crushed sleeping pills into your pasta, and your drink."

"Doooo–don't you dare touch...him, don't you dare hurt our s...son." She slurred with a raised pointed finger as her body began to succumb to the drugs, her consciousness slowly drifting away.

"I'm sorry, Donna, but I have to make this right. I know, given time, you'll understand why I am about to do what I'm have to do. I just hope you can forgive me."

"I will never..." And with that, Donna slipped to the floor. Asleep. Peacefully. Paul sighed with sadness that it had to be this way but still, he had to sort this out. Soon enough, Paul placed his gentle wife on their sofa to sleep. Stroking her hair, he placed a loving kiss on her forehead. "I love you," he whispered to her, before leaving to finish what they had both started.

Picking up a large knife from the kitchen, Paul readied himself, opening up Reggie's crib to face the monster within. The child was awake now and hissing with his snake tongue. Lifting the knife up high, Paul said, "This is for Reggie." He plummeted the knife down toward the infant...

*Sometime later…*

Donna stirred, awakening from her slumber. She hastily brought herself to her feet as she stumbled about to save her son. She peered over to the crib to find it open and empty? Seconds later, she saw a pair of feet, in a pool of, what appeared to be, blood. As Donna carefully walked around the table for a better view she gasped in shock to find Paul, a knife still in his hand. His throat had been practically torn out. He was dead.

To her surprise, Donna felt nothing. The man she considered, for most of her life, to be her true love was dead and she felt nothing, only emptiness, as she gazed down at his lifeless sack of a body. Why was that? *Was he not her true love after all?* her still dizzy head wondered.

A sudden scuttle rattled up and into the crib, Donna's hand clutched her chest in fear. Steadily she moved closer and, looking in, she could see her one true love. Her baby boy. The brute on the floor had tried to kill him and failed. *Thank God*, she thought. Gazing down she saw those slowly blinking, pale baby blue eyes staring back up at her, soothed. Lending a finger, the mother stroked her son's heads as he purred from his bloodied jaw. Donna looked down at Reggie, her one and only true love, and asked a simple question that only the mother of a monster could, "Now what am I going to do with you?"

And with that, Reggie seemingly attempted a human smile. In turn, his mummy, looked down on him, adoringly from above, sealing their twisted love forever...

## CHAPTER THREE

"The things we do for love, am I right?" Anna commented, as her cold eyes looked towards the flames.

Luke laughed. "Oh a zombie, vampire, baby monster, how original."

"It sure is that."

"I'm impressed." Luke's fiddled with his fingers.

"Thank you," said Anna replied, turning back to face him, the amber glow illuminating her face.

The young man pondered. "Tell me, would you bring someone back from the dead, if you could that is?"

"Me?" Anna asked in surprise. "I've got no one to bring back."

"Oh?" Luke frowned, leaning in closer. "How come?"

"I, erm…was born an orphan. Yeah." Anna's throat found itself swelling with years of repressed heartache. "My parents didn't want me. They left me in the street, outside the orphanage. I've never had family or friends, not really, not real ones."

"No, Anna, you must have friends," Luke insisted with sincerity.

"Not really, I've moved around from place to place. I've met a lot of fake people but no one has ever stuck around. It's always just been me." She sighed, though not unapologetically. "But I prefer it that way to be honest. There's no one to slow me down. If life has taught me anything it's that self-preservation is the only thing that really matters." Her forced smile said she believed this was the only true fact in life.

"Indeed!" Luke agreed, studying her closely once more, while sipping his now cold tea. "You're a complicated girl, you know that. Hard to read."

"No, I'm not. I'm a simple girl, I know what I want and I go for it, that's all."

Luke's head tilted to one side, like a curious pup. "And what is it you want?"

"I'm not sure? No one has ever asked me that?" Donna mused, not quite sure how to answer. "I guess just a shot, a chance at a future," she said, knowing there was no better gift from life than a future, a true future, unmarked and unchained by other negative circumstances.

But Anna knew that was not a life for her. Not one she would ever see anyway. Clean of sin and her past. Luke observed the hint of uncertainty as she turned back towards the fire. A flicker of doubt crossed Anna's mind and tears began to form, threatening to trickle down her cheek. Anna forced herself back to the present. Her guard back up. It was fascinating to watch her aura mould in the moment.

"What about you?" she asked. "Would you bring anyone back?"

"Me? No. Never." Luke giggled. "I believe very much in keeping the balance. Resurrection would only screw that up, I think so anyway. Life, death, the afterlife, whatever? They are not things to be meddled with. Who are we to play God? Who knows what you could wind up doing?"

"True, if such things were possible that is." Anna's eyes glazed over.

Luke's long legs stretched out as he stood tall, slowly pacing his way toward a window to look out into the woods and the night sky. His pale reflection shimmered as a thought occurred to him. "Hmm…you can tell a good story, Anna, but not a scary one."

"That wasn't scary?" Anna said. "You're telling me the crazy doctor, zombie vampire, baby monster experiment wasn't scary?" Her nails dug into the arms of the chair.

"No, it had no finesse. No subtlety to it." Luke said, turning to look in her direction. "Jump scares aren't creepy, they're cheap and tacky." He walked back over to stand in front of her.

"Oh really?" she said, clenching her fists.

"Yes," he said, resting his arm on the mantle, casually. "Your form of fear is like a hammer, blunt. But real fear is a thin, subtle blade. It creeps up on you, it lingers, sometimes you don't even feel it, until it's too late." He paused, then added, "In stories that is." He moved across to rest his strong hands on his chair.

"You're saying I'm like a hammer?" Anna rose to meet him face to face.

Luke grinned, stepping closer to her, in front of the raging flames. "I'm saying, from what I can tell, you are a fighter and I like that about you." His neck leaned in. "I like a girl who knows what she wants and goes after it with all she has."

Their faces were centimetres away, and they took a moment to breath in each other's scent. The connection between them grew somewhat animalistic and primal, suddenly. Anna couldn't deny that she felt it, and strongly. Their noses grazed as the heat bathed them in heat, generating raw energy. The girl's emotions were now mixed. How could she carry on with her plan with this chap? The stirrings she was feeling inside were merely complicating her moral compass, or rather, her lack of morals. As Luke's lips began to part, Anna backed off in resistance.

"I'm just doing my best to constantly clean up the mess that is my life," she said.

"I can see that," Luke replied.

Changing the subject, Anna turned her attention to a creepy clown doll beside her. "What's this then? Another cursed object?" she questioned, folding her arms, somewhat disturbed by the terrifying toy.

Luke sighed, dropping his shoulders. "No, it's just a doll. A Chuckles doll to be exact, ever heard of them?" he asked.

"No."

"I'm not surprised, they had a limited run. Only thirty were ever made, and few exist now. The origins behind them are fascinating and, dare I say it, disturbing." He was clearly getting ready to weave another tall tale.

"Oh boy, here we go." She slapped her thigh and returned back to her seat, relieved for an excuse to move away from him. She acted as if she didn't care but, in truth, she was intrigued, by Luke and his stories.

Luke carefully picked up the doll in his arms as if it were his child.

"Get comfy, this story is a fun one. It's set in a small toy shop owned by a Mr Baker…"

## STRINGS CUT

Rain trickled down the glass window of Baker's Toy Shop on a stormy Monday morning. A nerdy toymaker named Toby sat tinkering with something, whispering to himself, at his desk. His boss John, Mr Baker, stormed in through the back office with purpose wearing the same dissatisfied, sour expression he always seemed to bear.

"Toby, have you seen our sales?" Baker exclaimed, throwing down a numbered chart.

"No," said the poor toymaker, adjusting his large, goggle glasses to take a look. "Why? A-a-are they bad?"

"They are manure, Toby, utter manure," Mr Baker exclaimed, his short, pompous frame shaking a little. "We are losing money, and it's all your fault!"

"M-my fault?" Toby squeaked, as he reached to administer his asthma pump.

"Yes!" the boss man fired back. "This toy store used to be full of kids! Not any more! You need to make something the kiddies want." His bloated sausage fingers shook.

"Well, it's hard." Toby said, retracting back like a bashful turtle. "Kids nowadays just sit in front of their iPads. I'm t-t-trying…"

"Try harder!"

The young toymaker licked his lips. "Actually, now that you say it, I have been working on something for some time now…"

"Good," Mr Baker said bluntly. "Make sure it's got the wow factor." The man then retreated back into his office as Toby continued to tinker on his project, muttering.

Shortly, a young woman entered the shop. Toby's attention was drawn, he knew her, better than most. The girl was pretty in the traditional sense, beautiful even, and she knew it. She had a large, busty frame and, today, was wearing a leopard print dress and sunglasses. Large earrings, that were practically Christmas tree ornaments, hung from her ears. The young woman swept inside in a fluster, pulling back her curled, golden locks. Not wanting attention but not wanting to seem rude, she said, "Hey, Toby."

The toymaker's face grew warm, lighting up like a cherry pie. "Oh hey, April. How are you?" he asked.

"Yeah, I'm okay." She smiled from behind her sunglasses, looking round in suspicion.

"Why are you wearing shades?" asked Toby. "Haven't you noticed the weather?"

April paused; she had always found Toby's awkwardness somewhat charming and also a comfort. "Oh, it's just a bit bright."

"It's raining?"

"Oh yeah, fancy that."

Toby stood and walked over to her with concern. "Is something wrong?" he asked in a caring voice.

Biting her lip, April rejected the thought, and turned away. "No. Nothing's wrong."

Lifting his hands to face her Toby asked, "May I?"

As he touched her, the girl nodded and winced. She felt shame begin to sit upon her as he proceeded to remove her sunglasses, to reveal a bruised eye of purple, green, brown and yellow.

"Jeepers creepers!" Toby gasped.

"It's nothing," April said. Manicured, pink, acrylic nails reached for the glasses, once again, to cover her shame, before she began sweeping the already clean floor.

Toby twiddled with his fingers as he struggled to speak up. "W-w-well, I hope you don't mind me saying but it looks like Steven has been getting…a little r-rough with you, again?"

"It's not his fault, he's just very passionate," April sniffed, continuing to look down at the spotless floor. "He gets swept up in the moment."

Toby's facial muscles twitched as he finally managed to spit the words he wanted out, "I-I-I know it's not really my place to s-say but…"

Abruptly, a man wearing a leather biker jacket strutted in; Steve. His confidence filled the room with the musk of toxic masculinity.

"Alright, babe?" Steve grunted, slapping his girlfriend's backside.

"Yeah, good," she said. "Thanks for asking."

The brute strutted up behind the poor girl, rubbing her shoulders harshly as she let out little wisps of air.

"Ah, no problem. I'll pick you up around about five then," he whispered in her ear, as if about to lick it.

Letting out a submissive giggle she quivered, "Okay, see you then."

Steve grinned at the response. This little mouse was in the palm of his cat paw, trained to perfection to his liking. He proceeded to kiss and bite April's neck until he noticed Toby watching, disgusted and yet enthralled by the display.

"Enjoying the show, freak?" Steve called out.

Toby panicked. "Oh no! Not at all…"

"Good," said Steve, kissing his woman on the cheek. "See you later, babe."

"See you later," April replied with a wave as he left, banging the door shut behind him. The noise alerted Mr Baker.

"Who was that?" he asked, hoping it might be a customer.

"Sorry, Mr Baker, it was just Steve," April apologised.

"Oh, not that guy," Mr Baker spat. "Honestly, April I don't know why you don't dump that creep and find yourself a nice boy."

Toby grinned cheerily to the side with no one paying him any attention.

"He's no good for you," Baker stated, seeing the shiner she had acquired from the angle of her face. "And look at that eye! Honestly, darling, I fear for you! What if he takes things too far one day? He's no good, that one."

"I know you think that, but you only see so much, Mr Baker." Her voice quivered with emotion. "He's good to me, in his own way. It's complicated."

"Hmm…seems it," Baker said, knowing his comments would fall on deaf ears. He spun round to see a gormless Toby watching April sweep.

"Toby, where is that damn new toy!" he yelled.

The young toymaker jumped, broken from his reverie, almost tripped on his large shoes. He went back to his desk to continue working on his masterpiece. "It's coming along, Mr Baker, I promise," he said.

"Better be," Baker replied, marching up to the boy and hissing, "I've seen the way you look at her. Get it out of your head, it's never going to happen."

Having had his dreams knocked down, the toymaker bent his head down over his doodles and tools. Toby glared after Mr Baker, as the man's fat, rear, waddled back to his office. Toby could him moaning silently to himself.

Toby fantasied about seeing Mr Baker, as well as Steve, get their due. Lost in the hellish twisted ways he would punish them both, Toby snapped out of his reverie when he felt a soft touch on his shoulder. April's touch.

"I'm sorry, for what Steven said. You're not a freak, Toby," she sweetly said, placing her sunglasses to one side.

"O-oh, it's okay, no d-damage done," he replied in a fluster as she skipped over to dust the shelves.

"You know Valentine's Day is coming up, do you have any plans?" she asked.

"No!" His arms crossed, crinkling his papers. "Why?" he asked, hopefully.

April shrugged. "I was just wondering, maybe it's about time you got yourself a girlfriend."

"Oh. Y-yeah, sure. About t-t-time I guess, yeah," Toby said, redirecting his focus on his work to cover his glowing cheeks.

"You'll find someone one day, someone who deserves you," April assured him.

The nape of the boy's neck sweated fiercely as he rubbed it. "We can only hope." And with that Toby clicked one screw into place and was done.

"All finished. Mr Baker!" he bellowed. "Ah I can't wait to see his face when I show him!"

"What? What is it?" Baker squawked as he entered.

"My new toy," Toby said. "I tell you this is going to be a game changer! This will revolutionise the way…"

"Okay then, come on! Get on with it!" Baker gestured impatiently.

"Right, I give you…Chuckles, the friendly clown." Toby unveiled a puppet clown doll. Polished to perfection. It was carved from the cheap wood of the local prison's hangman's tree that once sat in the violent blood-soaked courtyard. The plaything was expertly moulded, pale and strangely sinister with beady looking acrylic eyes and razor sharp features cut with utter precision. "Ta da!" Toby presented the doll with jazz hands.

April's fingers rushed to her mouth. "Oh my goodness! He looks so funny."

Toby's smile widened. "So, Mr Baker, what do you think?" he asked.

Mr Baker took a deep breath in and, without remorse, spluttered the word: "Crap."

"I-I'm sorry?" Toby said in confusion.

"It's crap! It's utter bull crap!" the man flamed. "I mean what is it?"

"It's a toy clown."

"Well, I can see that. But what is it?"

"A-a-a…t-t-toy?" Toby stammered.

"I don't see a lot of money here." Mr Baker sighed.

Devastated the toymaker buffered. "But, but…"

"'But, but…'" Baker imitated. "Listen, kids don't want weird looking clowns, they want gimmicks! Fidget spinners, mini finger skate board things, light swords. Not this. Get rid of it and start over. Think something better." Mr Baker knocked the doll directly into the bin below it.

"But I…"

"Not another word." The shop owner then returned to his office.

Crushed, Toby's shaky hands picked up Mr Chuckles from the bin and carefully placed him back on his desk. He sat with his head in his hands. A pair of heels slowly clicked over to him. April rested a hand on his weary shoulder in support.

"Oh, I'm sorry, Toby," she said. "If it means anything I think it's great, very creative." She jingled a little collar bell on the doll with her nail and smiled.

"Thanks. Really," he said, looking at her before turning away bitterly. "I just wish *he* could appreciate it."

"Don't worry about Mr Baker. You're good at this stuff. Always have been. You have a kid's imagination! You were creative, even back when you were a kid yourself, when we were both kids, together," she said.

Her words soothed him and he began to regain his somewhat fragile composure. "Thanks! Really, that means a lot."

For the briefest of seconds, the pair shared a moment, a connection. Something unspoken passed between them as April giggled and broke away.

"Hey, do you want me to stay on tonight to help you come up with some ideas?" she asked kindly.

"Y-yeah, s-sure, that would be great." He jumped at the idea.

"In fact…" she said, pulling up a seat next to him. "Why don't we start now?" They both mirrored a smile as they began their journey into the world of toys.

The day rolled on and bled into evening, soon enough Mr Baker left the two youngsters to it. Relentless and tired they would not quit.

"And so if we made a rocket it could have like a spring activated missile that jumps out, what do you think? T-that could be fun, right? Or is it too much? I don't know? It's too much, right?"

Toby turned to find April fast asleep in her chair. "Oh," he whispered to himself as he grabbed his jacket and covered her. He glanced around to check that Mr Baker wasn't lurking in the shadows, before planting a kiss on her forehead and taking the chance to sniff her hair. Coconut, her hair always smelled of coconut. His favourite.

"Careful, Toby doing that, you never know who may be watching?" a playful voice called out.

Toby jumped and turned round swiftly in nervous agitation. "What? Wh-wh-who's there?" he stuttered like a machine gun.

Chuckles large, white-gloved fingers started to tap, one by one, and his neck creaked as he turned to meet his maker.

"Chu-Chuckles?" Toby said in shock.

"In the flesh…well figuratively," Chuckles said, before jumping down to the floor. Toby hastily backed away. Chuckles began a jagged, puppet-like dance forward. He was playing with his master, enjoying his reactions to every movement he made closer to him. Finally, bored of playing games, he moved back a little, propelled himself forward and jumped on to Toby's chest. Toby whimpered slightly and Chuckles mimicked him and slapped his face. "Come on, pull yourself together. I'm a damn toy!" he remarked sassily, sliding off his creator's chest to the floor.

"What-what do you want?" Toby asked.

"What do I want? Only to check on my bestest friend in the whole world," he said, before turning his sights to April, who was still sleeping. "Who's that? Not that babe, April?" The wooden toy saw Toby recoil and cackled as he played with his little red bow tie. "Oh, you devil!"

The toymaker rubbed his temples. "This isn't real? You're not real."

"This isn't real? I'm not real?" The clown mimicked, tilting his head as he knocked it, making a hollow sound. "Looks real enough to me."

At that moment, a bike roared down the road, coming to a halt with a screech of tyres just outside the shop.

"April, where the hell are you?" Steve bellowed outside.

"Oh dear," Toby murmured, feeling scared.

Chuckles jumped up to cover his mouth. "Ssh! This is gonna be great." He giggled as he slinked away behind the shop desk.

Toby hastily rolled April into the back office as Steve marched in, slamming the door behind him, clutching a bottle of half-drunk whisky in one hand. "April, where the hell are you?" he called out only to be met by a nervous Toby.

"Hey, Ste-Steven-"

"Where the hell is she?" the biker grunted.

"Who? April!"

"Who else, freak?" Steve said, pushing Toby against a shelf as he lurched over him with ill intent.

"Ah well, that's not very nice now is it, Steven," stated a naughty, childlike voice.

Steve spun round to be met by Chuckles, who was sitting smugly with his little wooden legs crossed over.

"What the hell?" The bully frowned in confusion.

"Didn't your mother ever teach you any manners?" A black wooden brow rose. "Let's start with introductions. I am Chuckles the friendly clown." He bowed theatrically as Steve blew out a loud puff of air.

"The shit is this?"

Chuckles head tilted in a cute way as Toby attempted to reach for the clown. "You look sad, maybe I can cheer you up?" The doll grinned.

Reaching again for the wooden animated toy, Steve said, "Hey, freak, what the hell are you…?"

And with that Chuckles jumped on to Steve. He placed his wooden hands around the bully's neck and began choking him with hellish might. Chuckles wore a splintered smile on his face, as he choked the life from the thug. Toby tried to pull Chuckles off but to no avail.

Steve rasped. "Hey, stop…"

"Oh, come on, give us a nice big smile." The clown's eyes widened as the man's larynx snapped with a crack. Both Chuckles' and Toby's grips loosened as the toymaker stood mortified at what had just happened.

"Oh my God! Is he d-d-dead?" Toby asked, pulling at his hair.

Chuckles sat on Steve's chest and poked him. "Well, he isn't alive that's for sure."

"What have you done?"

"What have I done?" The toy questioned, somewhat insulted. "What have we done? You made me, remember?"

"You're r-right. Oh no."

"Ah, I wouldn't think too much about it, he was nothing but a lightweight loser! Now better hurry, you've got a lot to do."

"Me?" Toby's forehead creased. "What h-have I got to do?"

Chuckles walked over with rigid, stiff steps. "Hide the body, of course. I can't do it. I'm just a doll."

"Yet you could still strangle a grown man!"

Chuckles' stick arms moved stiffly from side to side. "Hmm…I know, life's not fair is it," he said innocently. "But think about it. With his death, you can have it all."

"What are you t-talking about?" Toby asked, sucking in hysterical tears.

"Well, with old knuckles here out of the way you can have what you've always wanted, your true love." Chuckles winked suggestively.

It took a moment for it to sink in. "No…"

"April!"

"No!"

Chuckles laughed, then continued. "But I would hurry, you need to clean up this mess, especially before lover girl in the other room wakes up."

"No, I will just tell her the truth, that it was y-y-you."

"What? Me?" He giggled with pride. "The toy clown? Yes, I'm sure that will go down a treat." His point now made. "Face it, pal, everyone's gonna think it was you. Best get on with what you've got to do."

"I guess you're right." Toby said, adjusting his spectacles.

"That a boy! You're finally seeing things my way. The right way. Exciting isn't it, you can smell it in the air, no?" He sniffed, turning to Steve's lifeless corpse on the floor. "Oh no, must have been bucko over here voiding his bowls."

"Ew gross!" Toby winced as he struggled to move the big lug's body while Chuckles watched. "Can't you at least help me mo-move the body?"

"Sorry, I can't, my joints, they're a little wooden." The toy laughed at its own joke, slapping its wooden thigh with a thud.

"Yeah, real funny!" Toby said sarcastically. He huffed as he pulled at Steve's leg, with little progress.

"Here!" the clown said, throwing Toby a rusty saw, which seemed to appear from nowhere. Toby caught it in bewilderment.

"What am I s-s-supposed to do with t-this?"

"I don't know, clean your teeth with it?" Chuckles mocked. Toby plainly didn't appreciate his humour. "Oh for the love of… Cut him up! You know, make him more…portable."

Toby looked at the saw and, in his sleep deprived state, finally understood. "Oh right!" In a strange way, the clown was finally starting to make some sense to him.

As the toymaker began sawing off Steve's limbs, one by one, a door creaked open. Mr Baker stood in his pyjamas, flabbergasted by what he saw before him.

"Toby, what the hell is going on?"

The boy stood, blood dripping from his hands. "M-Mr Baker, it's not what it looks like."

"Oh my goodness…what have you done?" As Mr Baker turned to run, Chuckles jumped up and hit the man in the back of the head with a toy mallet.

"Nice to beat you." The clown laughed manically.

Toby groaned, now strangely desensitised by the occurrence of yet another death around him. "Great, now that's two bodies to cut up and b-b-bury."

"Who said anything about burying them?" Chuckles grinned, caressing his bloodied mallet. "There's a mincer in the basement, you could always feed them to the dogs? What do ya say?" Toby looked up, still holding the saw, and smirked.

It was a new day, in every sense. Time had passed. Toby and April now ran the toy shop together. They were happy and healthy and content with each other's constant company at work. Toby's stuttering had ceased, and his confidence bloomed as he sold yet another Chuckles doll to yet another customer.

"Thank you, come again."

April entered the shop with wide full rouged lips, looking better than ever on this sunny summer day. Giving off an unshackled sense of relief, seemingly taller, stronger with a new found sense of freedom. Like a flower in bloom.

"Wow, that's the twentieth Chuckles doll I've sold today! Business is booming." Toby grinned.

"Yeah, ever since Mr Baker went missing," April mused with mixed emotion. "I just went to the station again. They still haven't found any sign of Mr Baker or Steven." Her face turned sad.

"Oh, I'm sure they'll turn up!"

"It's been weeks! I'm starting to think the worst."

"Oh don't do that! You'll only stress yourself out." Toby said, walking round the counter to her. "Look, we can do what we want." He tried to amuse her by playing with some of the toys. A car and a spaceship flew and rolled around up her arm and shoulder with sound effects. She let out a little laugh. Then she recalled her worries again and sighed.

"I just wish I knew what had happened to them. For peace of mind if nothing else," she said, taking a seat up against a shelf. "I shouldn't really say this but ever since Steven left, I've been kind of glad; relieved. With both of them gone, in fact, I feel free. Free to pursue...other options."

Toby's cheeks tingled and he licked his lips as he perched on a seat beside her.

"Would knowing what happened to them really ease your mind? No matter how bad it may be?" he asked.

"Yes, I'd give anything to know."

"Really?"

She nodded. "Really, why do you know something?"

Toby thought for a while before answering. "Well, you know Chuckles," he said carefully.

"The clown doll we've been selling, yes, of course I know him," April replied, nudging him a little.

Toby hesitated, looking down at his large shoes, hoping for a degree of comfort as he quickly got on with saying: "He killed them."

There was a deafening silence and then a chuckle from April. "What?" she questioned, believing him to be joking, fooling around with her.

"He killed them," Toby repeated, somewhat doubtfully hoping she would understand.

April grinned. "Have you been drinking?"

A flurry of emotions hit the toymaker and he somehow garbled together a sentence. "It's true, but don't worry, I won't let him hurt you. I won't let anyone hurt you. I…" Toby paused then revealed, "I love you, April."

She let that sink in for a moment, looking into his foolhardy eyes and towards his swelled up, plush cheeks that now were as ripe as a peach. "Are you being serious?" April questioned.

"Yes, I have always loved you," he admitted, laying his heart out bare to her. Her thoughts and reaction were as yet unclear, until her neutral confusion morphed into a smile, much to Toby's surprise.

"Aw…and I love you too, Toby."

He exhaled the breath he had been holding, feeling relieved. "You do?"

"Well, of course I do, you're my twin brother," she said, bumping his shoulder playfully with her fist. Toby's heart sank. "Of course I love you. But right now I have to say you're sounding a little crazy. A killer doll clown murdering Mr Baker and Steven, I mean if that was true where are the bodies?"

"Oh I put them in the mincer and fed them to the dogs," said Toby, without thinking, hoping he could sway her with his utter devotion to her.

"Yeah very funny," she scoffed.

"It's true. I did it for you. To protect you," he explained, now on his knees before her. "I love you!"

April frowned, retreating back from him slightly. "Right, you're starting to worry me now."

"I've always loved you," he said, unashamed, his face contorted with untethered emotion. "We've always been together, and we always will be together. We deserve each other. Please…" He rose his arm to try and caress her cheek.

Are you seriously not joking right now?" April asked, knowing the answer by his reaction. On the verge of tears and disgusted to her core, she repelled his advances. "You're my brother, my twin brother!"

"I know, I know, but you can't deny the connection between us…"

"Of course there's a connection, we're brother and sister. You're sick, Toby, sick! Oh my God! You need help!" she yelled across the colourful store, almost gagging at the thought of them before coming too. "I thought you were different, I really did, but you're not, you're just like the rest of them! Mr Baker, Steve, you're a bully! And to be honest, I'm really sick of being bullied!" She ran over to the phone and picked it up.

Toby frowned. "What are you doing?"

"Calling the police, the psyche ward, anyone! To tell them what you've done. Whatever it is you have done!" April yelled, dialling a number with her nails.

"No!" he whimpered sorrowfully. "Don't do that."

April ignored him and continued dialling.

"Don't," Toby cried, grabbing her tightly.

"Get off me!" April screamed.

"No! I'm s-sorry…"

"Toby! Stop it! Let me go!"

"I-I'm so s-s-sorry…"

The toymaker began to strangle his sister, his lifelong lover, out of with resentment for her and himself. She grabbed his hands and attempted to batter him off as she rasped for oxygen. "Get off!"

"I love you," he whispered to her as a tear trickled down his cheek.

"No!" April silently screamed as her knee jerked upwards to kick him in the crotch, causing him to recoil in pain, before she punched him hard in the jaw.

As April ran to the door, she felt a harsh hand clamp around her ankle, pulling her and causing her to topple over. As she rolled to face her attacker, she could see the clownish demonic madness on Toby's face that clearly had made its way into his creation. All good artists put themselves in their work.

Toby was now on top of her, as she squirmed desperately. "Toby, stop, please."

It was too late, Toby was too far gone. As he wrapped his rigid hands around her brittle throat he squeezed with euphoric joy as he choked the life from her. His grinning malice was the last thing she would have in her mind as the endless darkness took hold. As her lifeless hands fell to the floor, Toby came too, realising what he had done.

"Oh n-n-no! No, no, no! W-wake up," he cried, allowing the sorrow that gripped his heart to take over, holding April's hand as he showered her with kisses. "Wake up, April." He began to hug his sister's lifeless body. "I'm s-sorry, I'm s-so sorry."

"No, that's not true," Chuckles casually chirped in as he strolled around the counter with a swagger.

"This is your fault," Toby growled.

The clown bowed. "Guilty!"

The brother gritted his teeth together hard. "You're a monster!"

"Pots and kettles," the clown replied.

"What are you t-talking about?"

"Haven't you figured it out yet?" the doll asked a blank faced Toby. "Oh boy, you really are as dumb as you are pathetic, and boy, are you pathetic." Chuckles words twisted like a knife. "I didn't kill Mr Baker and Steven. It was you. It was always you." He marched toward his confused master. "Like you said, I'm not real! How could have I killed them? I was merely the voice in your head."

Toby's chest tightened. "No!"

"Oh yes! You may not want to face the truth but, as we all know, we can't always get what we want, now can we."

Chuckles left Toby alone to suffer in his grief and madness, cradling his sister's empty shell of a body as he wept for her and for himself.

*Six months later…*

Now in a new setting, Toby was beginning to come to terms with his mental state, finally. Sat in a padded cell in a tightly-fitted straitjacket gave him time to ponder the many mistakes he had made. It was his hell and his haven. Muttering to himself gave him comfort; it could drown out the other voices in his head. All except one; Chuckles, his one visitor in the mental asylum.

The clown suddenly appeared atop the security camera mounted above the door of Toby's cell. "Don't worry, Toby, you won't be in here forever," Chuckles promised. "We still have work to do."

Toby shook his head frantically. "N-no, no, no! No m-m-more!"

Chuckles cackled in amusement, swinging his legs from high above, riding the camera like a pony. "Sssh!" he silenced and calmed his maker. "Well will you look at us two crazy kids in here, why we practically deserve each other."

Toby's eye twitched at the thought.

"Now give us a nice big smile." Chuckles grinned down at him sinisterly as Toby did just that back, back up at the camera for all to see. Toby's untamed madness was on full display. There he was, alone but not alone, until the bitter end. Trapped forever in his own mind…

## CHAPTER FOUR

"And that proves love kills far more than hate, and makes madness thrive and monsters of us all," Luke mused solemnly as he carefully placed the Chuckles doll back where it belonged. Anna let out a loud, obnoxious cackle that rippled off the wood timbers.

"Are you serious? That was the twist? He was insane? The clown was in his head the whole time?" she questioned in disappointment, her confidence growing by the moment.

"Well, yeah?" Luke spun in surprise. "It's a true story."

"Yes, but not a scary one. God, it might just as well have turned out that he had been dreaming it up the whole time. Clowns aren't even that scary."

"Not for you maybe," he replied.

"Not to anyone, not any more. They're outdated. Give me a zombie baby any day."

Luke thought for a moment, then asked, "What are you scared of then, if not clowns?"

"Oh, I don't know." The young woman dismissed the question, retreating behind her fingers as she combed her locks.

"Come on, there has to be something," Luke pressed, walking towards her.

"I don't know, I guess I don't like uncertainty," Anna admitted. She paused, then added, "But not horror movie monsters or anything."

"Never?" Luke asked, staring openly at her.

"No! Never."

"Interesting…" Luke grinned cheekily, breaking the tension. The look disturbed Anna. He did have a way of getting under her skin, but then again, so did a tick or a spider. The difference was he was no threat, or a parasite for that matter. "Boy, I feel like your shrink," he added soon after.

A streak of light pierced the room, white and bright, accompanied by the roar of thunder. It crashed down with a fierce rumble that hit the core of the earth below them, causing everything to shake. The pair looked around to make sure they were safe. That nothing had been hit. It hadn't. They were safe from the strike. For now!

"That's quite enough of that," Luke said, moving over to the radio to take his mind off the storm. Turning it on, the song 'Devil Woman' began to play. The hospitable boy moved comically, in time to the music, to lighten the mood. Anna laughed reassuringly as he danced, if that was what you could call it. Cringeworthy and awkward, his moves soon burnt out, along with his terrible rhythm. He bopped over to the window as yet another flash of light and roar from above sent a shiver down his spine, exciting his senses. Anna kept her gaze fixed on her prey; Luke.

"Ooh look at those clouds, something wicked this way comes," Luke said, looking out the window and giggling. He spun round cheerily to face his guest. "Oh I love a good storm! The crashing thunder. The electrifying lightning. The devastating wind. So…exhilarating." With that, he glanced upwards to check the clock on the wall. "Eight o'clock." His brow furrowed with apparent concern. "They should be back by now," he said.

"I'm sure your family will be return soon," Anna said in a soothing tone, trying to appear empathetic. "Maybe they've had to shelter from the storm."

"Yes…" He nodded, reclining back in his seat. "I think I'll give them a call to see how long they'll be."

Luke took out his mobile and tapped on the screen. "No reply, that's odd." He repeated the process. Still nothing. "They're not answering," he said, looking worried. He tried a third number and, this time, left a message. He then put his phone back in his pocket and spoke to Anna. "I might as well get on with dinner! You'll still stay and have some, won't you?" Luke asked, a slither of concern discernible in his voice.

Anna smiled. "Yeah sure! Might as well. What is it?"

"Roast beef," he replied, wedging the kitchen door open. "I'm just gonna get it out of the oven, I don't know about you but I'm starving." His face relaxed and he returned to his usual light-hearted self, as he disappeared into the kitchen to whip up the most succulent of dishes.

"Yeah," Anna replied, checking to see if he had left. "Can't tell you how hungry I am…ravaged even." She slipped out the knife she had been hiding in her sleeve. It glimmered satisfyingly in her hand but she was now conflicted. Above, the skies cried and brought down more claps of lighting as the storm outside continued to rage. Anna remonstrated with herself. The night was still young and she had work to do…

*A little later…*

Luke and Anna sat together eating a feast, each with a glass of wine, which Anna knew she had to be careful with, she never drank to get drunk. The taste was fruity and rich, causing her cheeks to flush with a feverish colour. They sipped and nibbled in silence, giving Anna time to observe Luke closely. She noted his precise way of eating. He smiled at her, causing her to freeze in both motion and thought, disarmed by the charm aimed her way.

'Calling Occupants of Interplanetary Craft' played on the radio as they enjoyed their food. The meat was medium to rare and was just the right amount of juicy, causing all of Anna's senses to heighten more and more with every bite she took. She salivated and savoured every morsel as she sat on her dagger, ready for the opportune moment to strike. *Not yet*, she concluded, she was enjoying her meal too much to tear herself away from it now. Well, unless that was to get more. Anna hadn't had a meal like this in some time. She was used to fast food take outs in her line of work, microwaved meals if she was lucky, but not this. This was something special; home-cooked food. It made her feel special. Luke, in fairness, also made her feel special.

This was all very strange to Anna. She was a girl who understood a person's motives. Dinner with a man often meant he wanted something from her, but Luke seemingly didn't. Being as sharp as a razor, she was used to seeing through people, and avoided such pleasantries, but even she couldn't had to admit to herself that she liked it. There was an ease in Luke's company she had never found with anyone before. It felt so natural and she realised she enjoyed being with him. But it wouldn't last forever. None of her relationships ever did. Besides, he was just a job, collateral damage, but for now Anna decided she would just herself, for the time being anyway. Anna couldn't let emotion get in the way of business, and for her, business was survival.

"So what do you think?" Luke asked, inviting critique. "How is the beef? Not too gamey?"

Anna looked up, breaking away from her pragmatic thoughts. "Oh perfect, the beef is perfect," she said truthfully, taking a gulp of richly flavoured wine.

The young man wafted his fork as he chewed. "Does any of it taste different at all?"

"No?" Anna paused. "Why? You're making me worried," she laughed.

"Oh no, it's not poisonous. Damn economy! It's too expensive these days," Luke joked. "I kid! Sorry, humour has never been my forte. No, I just like to use a lot of seasoning that's all. I'm quite the cook, well, try to be."

Anna's eyes twinkled with humour. "I can tell," she retorted, carving into generous slice of meat.

Luke saw the time was almost ten o'clock. He was now worried. "Oh boy, it is getting late, I wonder where they can have got to?"

"I'm sure they're fine, Luke," Anna said casually, when in truth she didn't care. "They must just be caught up somewhere."

"How can you know they're fine?" he asked.

Anna lifted her glass, swirling the liquid, as she tried to dislodge a bit of debris from between her teeth. "I don't know, I just, have a feeling. But if you're that worried you should try and call them again," she suggested, returning to her wine.

"I guess I should, just to check that they're alright." Luke placed his napkin to one side and got up to leave the room, taking his phone out of his pocked. "Excuse me."

"No problem. Take all the time you need."

It was time to make her move. Suddenly, Anna sprung up like the black mamba she was, removing a small packet of powder from her pocket and tipping it into Luke's wine. She mixed it with a spoon and looked to see where was, before returning to her dinner.

Shortly afterwards, Luke returned looking confused.

"Weird they're still not answering," he said in slight anguish. "None of them. Their phones are all going straight to voicemail."

"Maybe they have no signal or something?" Anna said, the floral scent of wine on her breath.

"Maybe, oh well, I suppose they may have got lost checked into a motel or something, something like that. Best not stress, let's finish our meal," Luke said, sitting back in his chair.

Anna watched closely as he continued to eat, not taking even the slightest notice of his glass of wine. Impatience finally took over and the femme fatale thought of a way to get him to drink.

"Perhaps we should make a toast?" she said, with a hint of malice.

"To what?"

Anna lifted her glass as she struggled to come up with something. "Ergh...to new friendships," she said eventually.

"Ah yes, that sounds nice," Luke agreed. He went to lift his glass only to knock it over, smashing the glass and spilling every drop of wine over the table. Luke jumped up and Anna tried to hide her annoyance.

"Oh God, I'm such a klutz," Luke said, as he mopped it up with his napkin. "My mum is gonna kill me!" He took the dripping napkin and broken glass away to the kitchen, returning with a fresh glass of red wine in his hand.

"There we are," he said, seated once more, as he lifted his drink to meet hers as initially intended. "To new friendships." He clinked his new glass against Anna's and she masked a smile of irritation as they both took a sip of wine.

"So, I believe it's your turn to tell a story now," Luke said, breaking the silence.

"My turn?"

"Yes, I did the last one. So now it's your turn."

"Oh so this is a thing now," she joked in a mocking tone. "Okay, fine, let me think."

Listening to the song currently playing, Anna recalled a story she was once told. "Okay, this song makes me think of one. It's a bit different but…you'll see…"

## DON'T LOOK UP

Leaves crunched underfoot beneath an autumn sky in the woodland wilderness. The song 'Calling Occupants of Interplanetary Craft' blared through one young hipster's phone as he scratched his wiry beard, leading his group of friends forward into unknown regions of nature's twisted and grassy wonders. Their bulging backpacks jangling as they moved onward.

Part of the foursome, comprising of two couples, was Josh, a confident young man with a strong jawline, black hair and six foot stature. His girlfriend, Gemma, a colourfully dressed woman with a strut to her walk, attempted to take photo after photo, with filter after filter, ready to upload to her social media.

Elliott, the hairy goofball, was in front with his girlfriend, Karen, the redheaded, ponytailed, uptight hypochondriac.

"Jeez, can you turn that crap off," Josh groaned, having listened to the song play for four long minutes.

"Yeah, come on, hun, it's like Satan's Spotify playlist," Karen said, rubbing his arm. "It's awful."

Elliott threw his arms down as he stopped the track. "How many times do I have to tell you light rock is soothing," he whined.

"More like shit," Gemma came back at him. She, Josh and Karen all laughed, much to Elliott's annoyance, as they trudged on through fallen debris.

His fingers pressed the phone, playing the song again in rebellion. "Yeah, sure, laugh at me, you always do anyway," he said, sulkily, moving further ahead of them all.

"Come on, man, stop being such a drama queen," Josh called after him. "Just chill, you're out for a fun weekend camping with two of your closest friends and your girlfriend, lighten up a little."

"Yeah, and turn that crap off," Gemma said. "It's my birthday weekend, so my rules."

Rolling his eyes, Elliott submitted. "Fine."

As the song cut, the birds chirped high above through the intertwining web-like branches, blocking out the sky. The wind called out like a baleful whisper. Gemma took note of the sounds of nature, putting the birthday messages on hold, as she lowered her phone screen for a moment to take it all in.

Josh felt in his pocket for the ring he had on standby to propose to his love. He had been putting this off for far too long out of sheer anxiety and fear of rejection but the time had come, it had to be this weekend, but exactly when he was unsure. He knew he would have to wait for the right moment to present itself, when they were alone, and seize his opportunity.

Elliott continued onward, with a lowered head, hoping to find some variant of insect that he could crush underfoot with his boot. Karen pointed to a circular, grassy, bare patch ahead.

"Ah there's a nice spot, we can set up camp there," she said and soon they were lowering their ruck sacks and preparing their camp.

The day dissolved into night. The stars glimmered and glittered serenely, shining down upon them all as they sat around their sparkly camp fire toasting marshmallows on sterilised wooden sticks – to soothe Karen's germaphobic mind. They chatted and reminisced, as they sipped warm booze out of Josh's flask and guffawed into the night, exuding good cheer.

Elliott sipped from the flask. The liquor warmed his throat like healing honey. "Damn this is some fine whisky. Where did you get it from, Josh?"

"It was my grandfather's, it's been ageing for years," he revealed, grabbing the flask, as it was gently tossed back to him. "I'm not sure how old it is." The young man took a glug and he threw the metallic container back to Elliott.

"However old it's some good shit." Elliott nudged the whisky to his other half. "Here, Kaz, get some of that down your throat."

"No thanks," she said.

"Sure?" he questioned, rattling the drink. "It will warm you."

"I don't do whisky."

Gemma gazed up to the endless wonders that conspired above. "God, look at the stars. Aren't they beautiful?" she mused, curving her lips to form a smile. Josh loved that expression of wonderment; he found it attractive and endearing.

He shrugged his strong shoulders. "Just looks like a load of dots to me." He looked up by her side and she raised a brow at his short-sightedness before he grinned like the schoolboy he still was. "I'm joking," he teased as her light fist punched his chest playfully. "It is something." He nodded in agreement as they romantically viewed the skies together.

"I mean it's just endless isn't it? Who knows what's out there, waiting for us," Gemma said. She watched her breath leave her across the embers before feeling Josh's warm embrace snuggle up against her beneath a blanket. She felt giddy and lightheaded, not knowing if it was all the birthday attention she had received, the whisky in her system or the hand she felt caressing hers. Gemma's cheeks warmed with a feverish heat as she evaluated the artistry above with her lover and friends by her side. *Was this true happiness?* she wondered. *Was this as good as it was ever going to get?* Surely it was; nothing could be better than this.

"I want to treasure this moment forever," she said, resting her head against Josh's neck as they hugged, taking in the wonders around and the wonders above. His hand slipped down to feel for the ring in his pocket.

Randomly, out of nowhere, Elliott began to vocalise and strum a guitar with his Neanderthal digits. Plucking the strings and beginning to sing Marvin Gaye's song, 'What's Going On', like a strangled cat, to everyone's disdain, pulling the plug on the treasured moment for them all. They each looked at him, baffled with disgust.

Josh's brow furrowed as he retracted the ring away from prying eyes. "What the hell do you think you are doing?"

Elliott stopped strumming and peered up to them in confusion. "I'm singing a song, thought it would be nice?"

"Yeah, well it's God awful, man," Josh roasted. "I'm surprised the wolves aren't howling."

Karen's neck rose like a meerkat. "Wolves?"

"Yeah, and where did you learn to play the guitar anyway?" Gemma questioned with curiosity.

"Oh, he's been having classes, part of his quarter life crisis," Karen explained.

"I'm not having a quarter life crisis…"

"You are having a midlife crisis and no one wants to listen to Elliott's greatest shits," Karen snapped back, snatching the guitar and tossing it to one side as the other two watched and giggled beneath their cover.

Elliott screamed like a toddler. "Hey!"

"And who said romance was dead," Josh quipped.

"Can't you just appreciate the night sky?" Karen prodded her yeti of a boyfriend as he sat bewildered. "Look at it!" she commanded, pointing up.

"Oh yeah, look at that," he said, scrunching up his nose.

"Useless." Gemma shook her head.

Elliott huffed, blinking slowly. "It's just that I'm not into this sort of stuff like you guys. I just don't get…" He gestured around their woodland setting. "This nature stuff."

Josh broke away from under his cover and patted his friend's back. "Give it time, bud, I promise after this weekend you will be a nature lover for sure." He winked at Elliott, and reclined back against Gemma.

Karen hummed in thought. "I have my doubts."

"Hey, did you guys get some good pics of the crop circles by the old farm?" Elliott asked.

"Yeah, why?" Gemma responded. "Did you not get any?"

"Na, I was too busy applying mosquito spray to this one's back." He jerked his thumb towards Karen.

Gemma lifted out her glowing phone screen, illuminating her face, seeing all the notifications she had collected. "Want me to send them to you?" she offered.

"Yeah, please."

Gemma began to type furiously on her phone but recoiled when she saw a sudden and abrupt notification. "Damn, no signal or Wi-Fi." She moved her device around her in an attempt to bring it back to life.

"Wow! Imagine having no signal in the middle of the woods," Josh mocked.

"Shut up," she said. "Okay, I'll send them when we get home." She glanced again at her screen until she finally gave up and put her phone back into her pocket.

"Cool beans," Elliott said, adjusting his hiking boots.

A rustling sound came from a bush, behind them and their tents. Gemma's neck jerked round to look, peering into the camouflaged darkness that surrounded them. "Hey, did you guys hear something?" the intuitive girl asked.

Josh glanced around to where she was looking, concerned. "No!"

The other two listened, Elliott relaxed, and Karen anxiously. Their heads shook in response.

"I'm sure I heard something," said Gemma.

Grabbing a torch, Elliott shone it beneath his face, making it glow menacingly as he rolled his eyes back and said in an eerie voice. "Ooh we're being watched!" His fingers crept up towards Karen, who slapped them away.

"We probably are, to be fair, we're in the woods, after all," Josh said matter of factly.

Karen swallowed hard. "By what?"

"I don't know, it could have been a fox, or a badger, or even a wolf or bear." He ran his fingers through his thick black hair. "Who knows?" Josh shrugged.

"A bear?"

"Oh yes, they are often found in these parts." His tone remained nonchalant. "Regularly."

"Really?"

"Yes, there have been lots of sightings." He nodded. "Do you know how many bear attacks there were here last year?"

"I don't know…"

"Go on, guess."

"I'm not sure I want to."

"Go on, it's fun."

"Erm? I'm not sure? Six?"

"Oh higher."

"Twelve?"

"Much higher."

Gemma gulped. "Eighteen?"

"Higher."

Her voice quivered. "Twenty?"

"Twenty-two," Josh replied. "Which is not a lot when you think about it."

"No?" Gemma questioned, looking around her fearfully.

"And, let's face it, there are worse ways to die in the woods. Bears would be a picnic. A pack of wolves could tear you apart. You could get bitten by a snake. Or hell, get raped by a hillbilly mountain man and then tortured and chopped up and made into stew." Josh laughed as both Elliott and Karen froze in horror. He looked at his watch and began to stretch as he yawned. He got up from beside Gemma and pulled her to her feet.

"Ooh looks like it's about time for bed, goodnight, you two." With that, they retreated to their tent, leaving the other two paralysed with fear as the fire began to dim. Owls hooted all around, making them skittish before they too scampered off to their tent not hearing their friend's giggles as they proceeded to snuggle and settle. Drifting off into a fast slumber.

An emerald haze of mist fell upon the camp soon enough as Gemma slept beside Josh. As the birthday girl dreamt, she tossed and turned, her expression ever morphing, like a block of clay, reflecting a range of emotions. With the moon shining down, a long-limbed, humanoid shadow cast itself upon the back wall of their tent, creeping outside. Strange noises could be heard, as flashes of light mirrored Gemma's movements, her muscles spasming as the creature outside drew nearer, ready to open the thin shelter.

"Elliott! Elliott!" A shriek echoed through the woods as Gemma shot up, gasping awake beside Josh who stirred also. His eyes stinging from the shock of being suddenly woken.

"The hell?" he murmured.

The pair stumbled out, struggling to see a hysterical Karen. Her shrill gave away her position in the dead dark wood.

"Elliott! Elliott!" she called out in a panic.

"Hey! What's wrong?" Josh questioned, drifting over with Gemma as he felt the safety of the cold metallic ring in his pocket.

"It's Elliott, he's…he's missing," she said, hyperventilating.

Josh frowned, rubbing his face. "Missing?"

"Well, maybe he's just gone to the toilet or something?" Gemma said.

"What for two hours?" Karen exclaimed, tears trickling down her face.

"Oh," Gemma responded."

"Maybe we should phone the police?" Karen wept.

"We've got no signal though, have we?" Gemma reminded her.

"Ah crap, I'd forgotten."

Josh huddled them all together, rubbing Karen's back in an attempt to soothe her. "Okay, listen, we'll find him. Right, we'll find him, together. He's probably tripped or something or had too much whisky. Don't worry, we will find him," he promised.

Karen nodded frantically. "Okay."

Josh briskly took charge. He grabbed the torches from their bags and passed them each one. They turned them on, shining their beams around the surrounding trees.

"As long as we stick together, nothing can go wrong," he said, rotating before picking an open route ahead. "Let's try this way."

And, soon enough, the three journeyed ahead on the search for their friend and Karen's boyfriend.

Forty-three minutes later...the woods had grown darker, more twisted and angrier. Noises were enclosing on them. Growls and grunts. Karen had gone from bitter concern to sleep-deprived anger and was swirling her flashlight around, trying to catch sight of any movement. Josh tried to remain calm and collected.

"Found anything yet?" he asked.

"No, not yet. I swear when I get my hands on that man I'm gonna strangle him to death." Karen's palm tensed tightly, clenching her torch hard as something rustled past them, which they missed by a blink.

Karen spun round. "What was that?"

"It's nothing, just leaves," Josh insisted, pushing on.

Gemma licked her lips, unsure how to say what she was thinking. "Maybe we should wait till morning, when it's light?"

"Wait a sec, what's that?" The young man shone his spotlight on a lifeless dangling limb. As Josh repositioned his beam he realised that it was a monstrous half stag, half pig, failed experiment, left to hang by its rotting intestines. Karen gagged as Josh and Gemma shrivelled at the sight of the unnatural display before them.

"My God," Gemma said. "What do you think did that?"

"I don't know," Josh said, his torch shaking in his nervous hand. "I've never seen anything like that before."

Another snarl was heard and Karen jumped in response. "What was that?" she asked, looking off into the distance. "Elliott?" she pondered, wandering away from the other two who remained entranced by the monstrous corpse.

"This is weird," Josh whispered.

"What do you think, Kaz?" Gemma asked. There was no reply, and she spun round to see her friend had gone. "Kaz?" She was nowhere in sight and every direction looked the same. "Ah crap."

Josh took Gemma by the arm and hastened her away, accelerating their search with a boost of adrenaline. "Come on, we can't lose another one." They half-jogged away.

Alone and paranoid, Karen frantically brushed past twigs, leaves, wriggling beetles and millipedes, some crunching and snapping underfoot. Calls spat out to her as she ran. She felt the veins within her pulsate, as if a temptation to whatever was circling and rustling around her.

"Elliott? Is that you?" She paused, listening for an answers, pivoting her torch back and forth. "Elliott?"

Suddenly, caught in her bright light, she saw a bundle of rags, of clothes even. Familiar ones. As she slowly stepped closer towards them she gasped in realisation; they were Elliott's clothes. Torn up and damp with a thick goo that lay all over the woodland floor. Lowering herself to pick them up Karen quivered in fear and distress, holding back her sorrow, before a large beam captured her with a deafening buzz, blinding her from above. She began to scream only to realise her shrieks were being muted. She was being risen up horizontally now, as if on her back. She felt her neck swing back to hit her heels, as her spine was forced to snap like a broken ruler. The pain was agonising. Soon every one of her bones were snapped and broken like toothpicks. She hung suspended within the science of the godly light lifting her up before the black took hold. Enough. Done. She was their plaything now.

"Kaz! Kaz!" Gemma shrieked, running through the endless woods. She was sure they were running in circles. "What is happening?"

Josh points his torch at the clothes.

Soon enough, Josh saw the flicker of light in the distance and ran towards it with Gemma. Karen's torch, left behind, still shining on Elliott's bundle of remains.

"Gem," he shuddered grimly. "We need to get out of here."

A roar of inhuman snarls and strange noises began, a hunt call that seemed to come from everywhere.

"What's that?" Gemma said, frozen next to Josh looking out to the distance.

"Nothing good."

The noises suddenly grew louder.

Josh's uncharacteristically silent demeanour spoke volumes to Gemma as he exhaled and then tried to calmly whisper, "Run."

Dropping their torches, they ran for survival. Josh and Gemma sprinted as fast as they could, trying not to catch their feet on anything jutting out of the breathing ground. The creatures were catching up fast. Josh grasped Gemma and hid her behind a large oak tree.

"What are you doing? We need to go," she mouthed silently to him.

"You go, get yourself out of here," he ordered with urgency as he reached deeply into his pocket.

Blinkered, Gemma stood confused. "What, no, I am not leaving you here."

"Just go, I can distract them long enough for you to escape."

"No, Josh…"

Grabbing her waist Josh pulled Gemma in tight, kissing her once more, for the last time. The world was spinning away, creating as a sweet psychedelic tunnel of love for them both. Their hearts were beating fast and together, as one, as they cherished it all, the good, the bad and the now. Placing his birthday gift into her hand, Josh pulled away, their hands drifted apart, the dream broken. Looking down to her palm, she could see the glittering, diamond star ring he had placed there; an engagement ring. A pained look crossed Gemma's face as she looked at Josh who caressed her now wet cheek.

"Go," Josh commanded. "I love you." Gemma mouthed 'you too' back to him before turning to flee, regretfully, with a broken heart.

Taking a deep breath, Josh accepted his fate as he jumped out, flapping his arms around. "Hey! Over here!" he yelled, drawing the monsters' attention as they ran full pelt hurtling toward him. He stood quivering on petrified legs at the sight. "Oh shit!" he murmured to himself, as he began to run, cold fear clenched his fast-beating heart.

As Gemma ran, blood thundered in her ears, as she clasped the ring on her hand tightly. She couldn't help but think how she had just left the man she loved to sacrifice himself for the love of her. She was so selfish. They should have stayed together. Maybe they could have figured another way out.

Whack! Before she knew it, Gemma had tripped and hit her head on a rock, causing her sight to blur and her hearing of the creatures' distant calls to distort. Delirious, Gemma brought herself to her feet, seeing a familiar scene. The camp site. Stumbling her way into the tent, she sealed herself in, cradling herself in the dark into a foetal position, rocking back and forth in soul trembling terror. She tried to focus on keeping herself quiet. She reached deep into herself, to place a layer of calm upon her fear, like oil on water. Opening her hand up, she gazed at the ring Josh had given her, but the mere sight of it caused her to well up once more. Somehow, she managed to bite back her tears and hold in her cries. Mustering up restraint, she placed the ring on her finger and watched it glimmer in the pale glow of the moonlight.

As a last desperate attempt, she grappled out her phone which now refused to even switch on. Frustrated, terrified, heartbroken and angry, Gemma threw the device away. And then, far in the distance, she heard shrieking, painful cries, tortured captured screams that echoed towards her, hitting her hard as tears poured down her face. Shutting her lids tight, she dreamt this would all go away as she silently cried, clasping her hands together as she knelt. "Please, please, please, I pray to you, I beg you! Please let me live! Please! I'll do anything just please!" she begged.

As she then opened her eyes she was surprised to find before her a warm fire burning brightly, one that revealed her companions sat around it, smiling at her. Elliott with his rugged exterior. Karen with her brittle demeanour. And Josh, of course, Josh, by her side, holding her hand. "Elliott? Karen? Josh? What's going on?" she asked, utterly confused.

"It's your birthday, Gem." Elliott said, sitting crossed legged.

They suddenly presented Gemma with a colourful birthday, decked out with candles that glowed her surprised face.

"Make a wish," Karen said, smiling.

Going to blow out the candles, Gemma hesitated. "Is-is this real? Are you all really here? Or just in my head?"

And with that, Josh took her smooth hand and kissed it with a gentle rub of his thumb. "Does it matter?" he said grinning, easing her strife.

"No," she replied, at peace now.

Leaning in, Josh caressed his lover's rosy cheek. "It's going to be alright, Gem, I promise." He paused, looking at her intently. "Now make a wish." He pushed the cake further towards her.

As the four began to hold hands in a circle they cherished the moment and each other, before Gemma bent down and blew out her birthday candles submitting herself to the darkness as the noise of the alien creatures slowly grew nearer.

## CHAPTER FIVE

"Aliens?" Luke cackled as he cleared away the dinner plates from the table. "I mean...aliens? Really?" His brow rose.

"Yeah?" Anna said petulantly.

Letting out yet another burst of giggles, Luke pottered off to the kitchen. "Sorry, it's just I wasn't expecting that."

"Yeah, well, who knows what's out there? We can't be the only living things in the universe, I can believe in aliens way more than I ever could in witches or boogie men."

"I suppose," Luke retorted, scratching his wrist.

"And anyway, who's to say they were really aliens! Hmm...maybe those things in the woods were just wild animals or monsters or something. Hungry for blood," she added, finishing off her glass of wine.

Luke smiled at the thought. "Hmm...most scary stories begin and end with blood don't they," he said as he moved past her to the fireplace. "With us, tonight, anyway."

Anna spun round, standing now, to bounce in the warm by the mantel. She grinned back at him, which he took note of.

Smiling to reveal a dimple, Luke paused, adjusting his glasses, preparing himself before speaking. "I read a theory once that all animals only want three things, to hunt, to eat and to mate."

"Well..."

"See, I don't believe that." He pointed a philosophical finger. "What about people, people who want power."

Anna sniffed at the thought. "Yeah...but what is power really? It's like money, just a means to an end."

"That end being?"

"I don't know. Food? Or sex?" Anna shrugged her shoulders, settling back in the arm chair, as she pondered more. "Hmm…maybe that's all any of life is, just an overrated mating ritual. Peacocking!"

"Or maybe the end goal is to kill," Luke suggested, his voice rising above the roar of the flames behind. "Money and power used to cover your hunts, your kills? Instinct. Maybe people climb the ladder so no one can see their trophies so high up. Maybe it is all just so they can hunt." He sat down gracefully opposite, a glimmer of something raw in his expression. "The most primal of animal instincts."

Pursing her lips in thought, Anna sprung up in recollection. "That reminds me of another story I heard, now you think the last one was too outlandish, well this one is very, very real and it all begins with a little screen, in the palm of someone's hand…"

## A DARK WEB SPUN

It was midday, unusually early for both youths, Sid and Andrew, to be up, let alone dressed by. Both sat on the latter's bed stationed within his dingy, dank, squalid room, watching the fuzz of a laptop screen that bore a small crack in the left hand corner with a beady camera hole that subtly sat mid centre of the top frame. Andrew leant into the screen, cackling without remorse, as Sid recoiled, squirming even, as a sickening acid brewed up from his large belly.

"Ah no, man! That's sick!" Sid cringed, behind open fingers.

Andrew's laughing grew as he leant back, pointing to the video they were watching. "Look, his head comes straight off," he screamed with hilarity.

"Na, mate, it's sick." Sid shook his spot-speckled head as he turned away.

"Ah, come on, you're telling me the guy who gets his balls crushed in a vice isn't a little bit funny? Or the woman who gets her hair lit on fire from fireworks? Or the man who spoons his eyes out, is not just a tad funny?"

"No, frankly, I feel it's content such as this that has completely desensitised our culture as a whole and made torture porn the norm in our entertainment industry and everyday walks of life," Sid explained in a soft voice to a muted Andrew who remained stunned by the comment.

"Wow!" he exclaimed. "That was a lot of words for you." Andrew paused, raising his crinkled eyes. "Look, listen, I'm always sat in this chair, handling code. Computers. It's my job, I understand the dark web, it's just code, pixels on a screen, nothing more."

"Yeah, but what if the police find out you're watching this?" Sid's heavy arm lifted to gesture at the crude display. "You know the government is aware of what we're watching, and all the hacks and firewalls you've managed to break through. They can see it all."

"Oh, please! You don't believe that shit?"

"It's a fact," Sid said, clumsily biting down on his own tongue.

"Well, I'm sure the government have better things to do than look at what I'm up to," Andrew assured his friend, who remained unconvinced. "Listen, what I'm saying is I work hard and, just like any normal person, I need to let off a little steam, watch some vines, funny videos some…naughty videos…"

"Yes…"

"And videos like this…out of curiosity. It's interesting." He shrugged. "It's educational."

"Let's agree to disagree."

A sarcastic yawn emitted from Andrew. "Party pooper."

Gazing at his ill-fitting watch, Sid said. "Oh, look, I gotta go. Brenda wants me to help move her nan's stuff out of the car." He got up with a struggle and began to waddle out of the room.

"Okay, man, you still good for Wednesday though?" Andrew asked.

Sid spun halfway out of the bedroom door. "Hmm…I'll let you know."

"Okay, see ya, mate."

"Bye," Sid replied, hopping his way inelegantly down the stairs, slamming the door shut behind him.

Andrew gave it a few seconds and sprung back to his laptop. Beginning type furiously and excitedly as he lowered his blinds, shutting out the sunlight, leaving only traces of lines, like prison bars across his room and face. He licked his lips, watching something most unsettling. Something not even he would share with his best friend...

Soon night fell, and the blissful tiredness of doing nothing took hold of young Andrew. Eleven hours of sleep he had managed to garner as he awoke to turn off his phone alarm. Creaking and making hangover noises, he slowly crept up. He grabbed his phone with a blurred degree of vision to see he had a notification. A new random follower he knew nothing of. *Becky Chaplin? Who are you? And why are you suddenly following me on Instagram?* he thought, examining her profile.

She was a blonde girl, with an hourglass figure, about his age, with striking features. His dream girl. *Almost too perfect,* he thought as he scrolled and zoomed in on an array of glamorous photos that held likes galore. *Oh wow! You are something. Think I will definitely be following you back.* He went to follow back, but then stopped himself. *Why would a girl like her follow me?* He pondered, before countering, *Ah, what's the har*m. His finger clicked as he sauntered up to his desk, carrying his mobile with him and plonking it down, letting the glow of his laptop awaken him further.

"Right let's check my emails…" he said to himself, dragging his mouse before he heard a ding coming from his phone beside him. Flipping over his phone, Andrew could see that all his photos were being liked by Becky. *Wow, okay, you work fast*, he thought, feeling chuffed. His heart fluttered a little as he wondered what to do next. How should he play this? Andrew was not one for subtleties. His lips pouted as he thumbs now scrolled through her profile, gazing at her perfect smile, tempted. *Hmm….well, it would be rude not to like some of her pictures in return,* The man/boy thought to himself as he began tapping relentlessly with his thumb, liking every photo. He regretted the move slightly, though not enough to rectify it. Instead, he placed the phone back down. Nothing would come from it, he knew. He returned to his emails before another ding came. Looking instantly, Andrew could see a message from her, from Becky.

BECKY: Hey!
"What is happening?" he questioned looking around as if he was on some prank TV show before slapping himself. "Okay, pull yourself together. Let's be cool. Erm…" Andrew struggled, but then soon began typing, deciding to keep it simple.
ANDREW: Hey! How you doing?
BECKY: Good thanks! Haha! How are you? xx

*Two kisses?* Andrew thought. *Not too keen but not too reserved. She's definitely interested. Okay, don't screw this up,* the boy fretted, feeling the sweat begin to form under his top as he began to formulate a response.

ANDREW: Good. Yeah, I'm good thanks! Haha xx

Becky instantly began typing a response, which kept Andrew on the edge of his seat.

BECKY: Hehe. Good, I like your pictures on Insta. You have a really nice smile! xxxx

*Wow! We're already on to compliments. Okay, let's see if we can take this a step further…*

ANDREW: Thanks, haha you have really nice eyes. xxxx

BECKY: Aw, thank you. You're so cute. xxxxx

*Five kisses, Houston, we have lift off.* Andrew smiled as he calculated his next response, going further and further as the day progressed…

Two days later, Sid arrived, having been summoned, his curiosity peaking more and more as he waddled in to meet his friend.

"Hey man, you alright?" he asked, seeing the grin plastered from ear to ear on his friend's face.

"Better than alright! I'm in love!" Andrew yelled, slapping Sid's shoulders as he yelped.

"In love?" Sid grinned, happy for his friend. Relieved even. "With who?"

"A girl I met online."

Sid paused, then continued. "Okay, I take it you've met her in person. Not just online, right?" he asked doubtfully.

"No, we haven't met, not yet," Andrew replied.

"Oh man," Sid let out, his optimism souring.

"No, but it's okay, she wants to meet me, tonight at the Revelation Hotel, down town," Andrew explained, his expression wide like a balloon, full of hope. "She's gonna wear a red flower so I know it's her."

"The Revelation? That place is a dump on the seedy side of town? Why does she wanna meet there?"

"Cuz, it's cheap. Maybe she likes seedy," he added, his brows rising.

"I dunno, this sounds bad to me, mate."

"What's bad about it?"

"You're meeting some girl you've never met at a run-down hotel in the crime-ridden part of town."

Andrew shrugged in hesitation. "Where are the cons?" he asked.

"It's fishy," Sid responded. "Did she message you first?"

"Yeah, saw me on Instagram. See." Andrew showed Sid a picture of Becky on his phone.

Jerking his head, he agreed. "Well, she is a ten out of ten, but her sliding straight into your DM's. It's weird."

"People do it all the time."

"Me and Brenda didn't, we met through friends, like normal people," he stated. Andrew mimicked a sock puppet talking endlessly.

"What if she's cat-fishing you? Like that TV show *Catfish*! What if that's not really her, what if twenty-two-year-old Becky is a forty-four-year-old man with a hobby of pizza parties for one?" Sid asked.

"Oh stop stressing," said Andrew. "I've already checked her other profiles." He scrolled through the comment sections. "Look she's got friends and family that comment and take photos with her on Instagram, Facebook and Twitter. She's legit. Can't you just let me have this? A girl likes me, can't you be happy for me!"

"I guess, I'm just trying to look out for you." Sid sighed, lowering his head as Andrew patted him on the shoulder in a caring way.

"I know and I appreciate it, but I can look after myself. Trust me."

Andrew mused the extent to which his friend showed loyalty. Warmed by it even now as he gazed upon him fondly. "Honestly, where would I be without you? After my parents died in that car accident you were the only one there for me."

"And I always will be," Sid promised and Andrew knew he would never forget this vow.

"I know mate," he grinned back at him as they both shared a moment. Having seen each other grow up from little boys to men. The years spent together, the memories they had. They shared them all, together. Their bond had been inseparable, until now.

Andrew had more than friendship on his mind; he needed something more. Something only Becky could provide, his dream girl. Slinking away from Sid, Andrew slung his overnight bag on to his bed which bounced under the force.

"Guess I better start getting ready," he said.

"Okay, well just be careful," Sid said, making his exit. "Phone me when you get there and if you need anything."

"Yeah, alright, Mum," Andrew teased.

His friend chuckled. "Have fun."

"Oh believe me I intend to," he said cheerfully as Sid left, excited but also scared for his friend as he began to get ready for his date night.

Heading down the seedy streets in a mini cab Andrew's nerves tingled with anticipation. He clutched his night bag with boyish zeal as the song 'Downtown' played on the radio. Paying the driver and hopping out with a spring in his step, Andrew arrived at the Revelation Hotel.

The exterior was decorated in a dirty, golden Aztec Art Deco style. As if a fallen empire was being held up by the surrounding peasants who lived in this part of the city. Each brick was stained with decadence and pain.

"Why would Becky wanna meet here?" he said to himself. "Oh yeah, it's cheap, that's why."

The grand sweeping doors emitted a sense of foreboding as Andrew entered with shaky determination. They opened to reveal a large, blood red lobby of sweeping grandeur. Walking towards the reception desk, Andrew noticed the place was empty, dry.

"Hello?" he called out before pressing the desk bell. It rang, loud and piercing, the sound bouncing off the walls. The silhouette of a long, slender woman emerged through a door behind the desk, accompanied by a constant banging of a stick with every movement against the floor that echoed hard and loud. A gold and black vulture skull cane was what the woman wielded, unmercifully, as she gracefully glided toward Andrew. Her features were sharp and narrow, harsh even. She had a dominating and intimidating presence. Her dark brunette hair was fashioned into a quiff, slicked back so tight that it looked like a helmet. She wore a black overcoat layered over a shirt that had a slightly skeletal X-Ray motif about it, making it appear as if she was rotting from the inside out. This was partially hidden under a layer of opulent, black Victorian-esque dress that she dragged behind her. She smiled coldly in Andrew's direction before making one final stab with the cane against the marble floor.

"Hello, I am the manageress, welcome to the Revelation. How may I help you?" she managed through her tensed jaw.

Andrew gulped loudly. "I'd like to check in please."

The manageress inhaled his scent, disgusted yet restrained. "Certainly," she said, banging her stick with every stride. She opened a large leather book. "What is your name, sir?"

"The reservation should be under Andrew Martin?"

A somewhat cruel grin came over her tightly drawn face. She then lowered herself down to read the book with refined precision. "Ah yes, right here. If you wouldn't mind signing our book." Her skeletal hand rotated the book carefully around for him to sign on a dotted line beside his name.

"Not at all," Andrew said nervously, picking up a chained pen by the side, looping his letters as best he could to appear sophisticated, yet failing nonetheless.

The manageress sneered at the attempt as she examined it. "Marvellous, thank you." She paused, closed the book firmly and slid it to one side. She then spun round and Andrew spotted a spine detail on the back of her jacket. There was something twisted and reptilian about the metalwork. It reminded him of the famous Latin saying *memento mori*, which his late uncle had taught him, making him briefly think of his own mortality and how time was fleeting. He then thought of happier things, like his date. Rotating back round, The manageress removed a set golden keys, that jingled lightly, and handed him one. "You will be staying in Room 237, sir." Andrew grasped the key from her claws and she gestured towards the lift. "Floor six."

"Thanks." He quickly made his way across the lobby to the lift.

"Oh and sir…"

Andrew spun to face the manageress, who was now standing immediately behind him to his slight shock.

"Enjoy your stay." She smiled, both her bony hands clasped tightly upon her cane.

Nodding frantically, Andrew replied, "Okay, thanks." He then entered the golden cage and ordered the lift upward as the woman watched him ascend. Like a cat watching a canary, her penetrating gaze was unblinking, making him feel more and more unsettled, even as he eventually lost sight of her. *That lady was freaky*, he thought.

Finally, the doors parted, revealing an unending hallway. A light above blinkered. Andrew began his journey along the sixth floor, passing endless numbers. It was so quiet, unusually quiet. Thirty seconds in, something hit Andrew. All the damn numbers in this place were mixed! It made no sense. He stopped for a moment to look at his key, to double check it: 237. He was between 394 and 178. It confused him. He was so completely bewildered, Andrew failed to sense or see the black-gloved hand reaching out to him from the slightly open door of 178. It extended out to grab the back of his unsuspecting head until the boy wandered forward to try and find his room, which he soon did. Room 237.

"Ah there you are," he said to himself, slotting the key in and turning the knob to his room. It was bland and deadly quiet, containing a bed, desk, chair, and a mirror hanging on the wall. The window had a lovely view of a nearby building's brick wall. It would do. Shutting the door, Andrew jumped and planted himself entirely on his mattress which felt hard and lumpy, unusual, but what was he expecting for the rate he paid. Inhaling the dust that filled the air, Andrew then whipped out his phone. *Hmm…no signal. Weird. Guess I will just iMessage.*

ANDREW: I am okay. No sign of forty-four-year-old men yet.
SID: Cool. I am glad haha.

Andrew wondered how long Becky would be. He began typing away, his tongue poking his cheek.

ANDREW: Hey, you here yet? xxx

The girl's typing icon appeared below.

BECKY: Nearly, gonna be about thirty minutes xxx
ANDREW: Okay! See you soon! xxx
BECKY: Can't wait! xxx

Andrew savoured the message. No one had ever said that they couldn't wait to see him. It made him feel wanted. Not alone. Smiling, he licked his lips in anticipation, then put his phone in his pocket. He lay tapping his belly looking around, bored. "Hmm…now we just gotta bide our time," he concluded.

Sticking his low grade earphones into his ears, he began to play music. Jumping up to do a little jig, he soon found himself to face to face with his reflection in the mirror. Not satisfied he started sprucing up his dark locks, then fixing his posture and expression. He wanted to seem kind, yet sexy. He tried out a multitude of looks until he finally gave up, feeling foolish, as he eyed up the mini fridge. He helped himself to a small whisky, the liquor warming his throat nicely. It coated him with liquid courage like a potion, instantly hitting him, making his muscles and senses feel lowered, safer, fuzzier.

Andrew decided to unpack his laptop, the appendage he could not live without. Sitting at the desk, he began to search for the one thing he knew would give him more of a tingle to get himself going for Becky. The one thing he knew he shouldn't do but it gave him a thrill nonetheless. Watching, he sipped his drink, before finally deciding: "This needs ice."

Andrew saw the ice bucket on the side table and shut his laptop. He stumbled over and read the pamphlet attached. 'Ice, just down the hall, help yourself'. *Don't mind if I do*, he thought, feeling the alcohol take more of an effect on him.

He opened the door, taking the key with him, his earphones still in. Andrew sauntered down the hallway, caressing the walls, on a high, as he finally saw the ice machine down one end of a particularly long corridor. Swinging his bucket and key as he approached, his music began to cut out. Andrew looked down to his screen to see it fluctuating in and out of signal. Frowning in frustration, he began tapping the screen and buttons on the side. Soon enough voices began coming through his headphones.

"Leave."

"Get out of here."

"Beware."

"Andrew."

The boy threw off his headphones, scared. His heart was palpitating and his forehead glistened with sweat. Then the lights began to flicker, until they completely blacked out everything. Andrew scrambled in the dark until he managed to find something to lean on, the ice machine, and leaning against it gave him a comforting chill, cooling his hysteria, but not for long.

As the lights glowed on once more, lighting the hallway, Andrew noticed there was someone, or something, watching him. A blackened, hooded figure wearing a disturbing, buzzing television screen mask. Frozen by the ice machine and the sight before him Andrew shuddered, unsure what to do. He fell back on his defensively kind-natured side. "H-he-hello?" he called out with no response but the sight of black-gloved hands clenching.

"Hey, can I help you?" Andrew asked.

The lights flickered again, on and off, allowing the figure to move closer, in time with the bulbs above, causing Andrew to jump back. "Hey I-I don't want any trouble…" Again, darkness and then light, revealing the figure standing closer.

A lump formed in Andrew's throat as he struggled to bring himself to say, "Okay, mate, you're really beginning to creep me out now."

Again, the lights whipped on and off, closer and closer the figure stood. Watching.

"I'm warning you!" Andrew yelled, standing still with dread until as yet another blackout hit. Andrew could hear his breath leave him along with thudding despair about what might come next. Expecting the worst when the setting was relit, he was surprised to find nothing before him. Nothing, just the empty hallway. He stepped forward to look at the muddled door numbers and bare walls. *Was this the effect of the alcohol? Surely not, but was it?*

Before another thought could be formulated, the bulbs flashed again. The hooded, masked figure lurched behind Andrew, one hand reaching for him as he yelped in terror. He dropped the bucket and ran for his life to his room. Fiddling with the key and knob, he could see the figure slowly encroaching toward him until, finally, the door opened.

Andrew swung in, locking the door behind. He even went so far as to barricade it with the desk and chair as he clawed for the room's phone. He dialled down to reception as a rhythmic banging began on the door. Andrew winced, then someone finally answered downstairs. "Hello! Reception! There is someone here! They're trying to get into my room! I think they're trying to kill me…"

The door was beginning to crack open. Andrew knew he had to act for himself. Grabbing a pair of scissors from his bag he hid under his bed, with his makeshift weapon, and waited for the inevitable. Until, finally, the door swung open. The figure's large boots cleared the barricades easily, skulking around the room. The boy under the bed clutched the scissors in sweaty palms and tried not to exhale too heavily. The figure moved over to the window to look out. Now was the time to act. Andrew stealthily crawled out from under the mattress and crept up behind the stalker, taking every step slowly but not too slowly. And then he jumped on the back of the assailant, who grabbed Andrew by the legs but not before he could sink his scissor blades into the masked figure's chest. Blood spurted out of the wound and the watcher fell down to the rough, stained carpet, clutching his chest.

Andrew stood over him, victorious and furious. The adrenaline and bloodlust testing the limits of what he could do. Was this what killers and torturers felt like? It was exhilarating he had to admit to himself. The boy had questions and he planned to get answers, no matter the cost.

"Who are you?" he yelled as the figure squealed like a pig beneath the mask. Andrew removed it, revealing a wheezing, stubble-bearing, middle-aged man. "Who are you?" Andrew again asked. The man began to cough up blood just as his hand lifted, unveiling something from his pocket. A red flower.

"What the…it can't be," Andrew whispered in shock and heartbreak. Becky was supposed to meet him wearing a red flower. Was this cretin his Becky? It didn't matter, for the stranger collapsed; dead. That was it. Andrew had taken a life, he had crossed that line.

His emotions were mixed. It was self-defence; he was being threatened and manipulated. Any court would see that. Did he actually feel bad for killing the stranger? No. Of course not. The man was a creep. Someone who, no doubt, would not be missed, no matter what his intentions were with Andrew. In fact, the victorious guest of the Revelation Hotel now lorded over the corpse before him. It felt good. He had put a piece of scum out of its misery. Andrew was, he regretted to admit, proud of what he had done.

The lights fell black once more, for a longer period of time now as Andrew spun, wielding the scissors. He was petrified for what would come next. And then, it did. He was surrounded by a group of hooded television mask faces.

"No," Andrew shouted. "Stay back!"

Again, the lights went out as the figures entrapped him further. They closed the circle as he spun round in fright. "What do you want from me?" he asked in anxious discomfort. "What is going on?"

"Well, isn't that obvious?" A cold female voice called out from outside his room. Then the steady clanking of that cane could be heard with every step closer before finally the manageress made her imposing entrance in the doorway. She wore a sinister smirk of pride. "You're about to die." She enjoyed watching the simple boy's panic, the confusion, as he gazed anxiously around at the masked figures. She gestured to them. "Oh these, they are just some of my friends. A particular clientele I cater for, you could say, the type that pay a lot of money for certain forms of…entertainment."

One of the figures slid back the mirror on the wall to reveal a secret camera hidden. It was, in fact, a two way mirror. But why? Andrew's face expressed his bewilderment.

"Oh, don't seem so shocked," the manageress sneered. "This place is scattered with them, as well as mics and secret passageways. Good for stalking, hunting or just scaring your prey. I'm not ashamed to say it certainly gives me a tingle."

And then it hit him. "You! You were Becky all along."

A cruel chuckle escaped her lips, before her 'business as usual' expression glazed back over. "Well, not me exclusively. My people. Becky is one of many online profiles we use, a necessary fiction," she said.

"So, she was never real?" His voice cracked slightly, heartbroken.

"No," she answered in an aloof and uncaring voice. "You see, people come to hotels, all the time. They arrive and leave, and if they go missing, no one asks any inconvenient questions. If they do, we act as if we don't know them."

"Wait…let me get this straight. You lure people here through online profiles to hunt and kill them?" he questioned. The head huntress confirmed this with a playful smile and a nod. "You're sick! Sick!" he spat in disgust. "But why me? Huh? Why me?"

"Why you?" She pointed at his chest, before moving closer, her cane banging on the floor with each step. "Yes, I was wondering when you'd ask that. You see, we picked you personally because we know what you've been looking at. What you were watching on the dark web." She paused for a moment, looking at his broken face. "Of the kids."

"No." Andrew shook his head. "No!"

Her tall frame leant in. "Oh yes, the videos you watch of those children when your friend, Sid, leaves your house, those sickening things. We know all about them. And I'm the 'sick' one."

"No, you have it wrong," Andrew whimpered.

"Do I?" A dark brow rose. "Deny what you like. We know the truth. We see and know everything. And soon enough we will make sure everyone who knows you, knows it too. Given time…." she trailed off.

"No!"

"Then again, no one barely knows you. You will hardly be missed." She paced in front of him with her cane. "Don't bother calling for help, no one in this building will help you and, besides, all the rooms are soundproofed."

Andrew felt fear poison his blood, boiling up to his skin. He took a deep hard breath and croaked: "Who…who are you people?"

The manageress crept closer, her eyes alert as ever, as she said to him, "We are the dark web."

And then Andrew's face crumpled.

The woman stepped back. "Make sure you leave the camera on; our overseas clients won't want to miss what comes next," she said as the circle tightened around Andrew. Panic swept over him.

"No! Please! No!" he cried out, pointing his scissors still.

As the manageress left, she paused to turn on the radio as 'Downtown' played once more. The figures readied themselves to snuff out the guest named Andrew Martin, for good. And before the boy knew it, with a quick slash of a knife, Andrew's stomach opened and burst outward like a rosebud, as he fell to the floor, clutching at his guts that stained the carpet red. More stabs came hurtling down toward his writhing body.

The manageress relished every slash and scream that came before she shut out the torment by closing the door. Taking a pause to lean on her cane in euphoric pleasure, she unveiled a 'Do not Disturb' sign that she hung on the door knob. The she moved on to meet her next special guest of the night, and many more to come.

A few days later, it was business as usual at the reception desk of the Revelation Hotel. The manageress was reading her guest list, which she cherished. Then, a heavily built young man entered, wearing a hoodie, gazing around, much to her displeasure. It was Andrew's friend, Sid. He wasn't a guest, she knew that much. He approached in a friendly manner.

"Hi, I was hoping you might be able to help me?"

She paused before answering, putting her book away. "Certainly, sir, what seems to be the issue?"

"My friend, Andrew Martin, he's gone missing, I haven't heard from him since he stayed here about a week ago? I was wondering if you knew anything?"

"Andrew Martin? Hmm…the name rings a bell. Tell me, was he here to meet a girl?"

"Yes, that's him."

"I believe I saw them together checking out the next day. I don't know where they went. They looked rather infatuated with each other."

Bringing his fist down on the desk, Sid exhaled. "Damn, so he's done a runner with this girl. At least she was a girl, I suppose," he added.

"Yes." The manageress grinned.

Tapping the desk, not sure where to turn next for answers, Sid smiled at the woman. "Okay, thank you very much."

"My pleasure, sir," she said to him as he began to make his leave. He stopped with a sudden thought and turned back around.

"I don't mean to be a pain, but would it be possible for me to see the room he was staying in?" he questioned. "I know I'm not a cop, and certainly don't have a warrant, but it would really put my mind at rest to know he didn't leave anything behind that might indicate where he could have gone?" His forehead creased as a plea.

She hesitated momentarily. A perfect candidate she realised. "Certainly, sir, I fully understand, better than most." She passed him the key, pointing to the lift. "Room 237. Sixth floor."

"Thank you so much, you're a life saver," he called out to her as he pressed the button.

"My pleasure, sir, I shall be up in a moment to help you look."

"Oh, thank you?" He watched the cage lower down to the lobby, just as he realised something was off. "Are you sure, you don't want me to wait? Seems a bit odd for me to just walk into the room before you?"

"No, by all means please, do, I won't be a moment. Be my guest, in fact be our guest." Her hand gestured warmly as she smiled.

"Okay, thank you," he said, entering the lift, clicking the button to the sixth floor. "See you up there."

The manageress gazed straight forward, her charade of a hospitable face dropped to neutral as her finger leant out, ringing the reception bell, indicating a new guest had just checked in and would no doubt fail, like the rest, to check out...

## **CHAPTER SIX**

Luke grinned, his fingers gripping into the leather grip of his armchair. "Ooh I liked that one, very dark and twisted." Anna suddenly opened up like a flower, relieving a little tension to receive the compliment, as Luke added, "Reminds me of the real life H.H. Holmes murder castle hotel."

"Yes," Anna agreed, somewhat surprised by his knowledge. "Very grounded though, not magic or madness or aliens or all kinds of screwed up monster babies! That's real horror! And that is always the most fun kind of fear." She smirked with relish, gripping the knife below her thigh.

"Yes, yes, I suppose you have a point." Luke nodded, as he collected his thoughts and rubbed his chiselled chin. "I liked it because it's true and links into what we were talking about earlier, you know about killing being a primal part of our DNA. It's fascinating, don't you think?" he asked curiously.

"Yes, it is. I think sometimes we forget that we are still all animals. Beasts of prey." Her tongue rattled like a serpent's tail.

"Indeed."

Anna smiled in saddened recollection as she gazed into the fiery pit beside her. "I remember when I was a little girl I saw a fox chase a rabbit, that rabbit, God, it ran so fast, it couldn't have run faster if it had tried. I remember watching as the fox bit into the rabbit's neck, snapping it. I ran over and managed to scare off the fox with a branch."

"So even back then you were a fighter."

Anna glossed over the remark. "Yeah, something like that."

"What happened?"

"I went over to look at the rabbit to see if it could be saved…but there was no way. It was dying, I could see the pain in its eyes, it was begging me to put it out of its misery, desperately." She winced in memory as Luke leaned in, enthralled.

"And did you?" he asked.

Taking her time, Anna got up. "No."

A painful pause filled the room. Anna was never one to lament on the past, what good would it do? Then again, she knew dreaming of the future achieved nothing either, no, Anna preferred to live in the now, in the moment. She focussed on merely surviving day by day, as best she could anyway. She hadn't thought about that memory in some time, it stabbed at her as she instinctively repressed back her emotions.

The wind, rain and lighting outside whirled in conjunction with each other, accompanied by the crackling of the burning logs in the fireplace. The warmth became oppressive but not unbearable. Luke could see the pain in Anna's demeanour, her soul. She knew she was not a good person, owned that even, but she did live with regret, to her disdain. Life is long when you live with regret, Anna knew, as did Luke, all too well.

The blond haired boy slapped his knees, moving the conversation along swiftly like a wave hitting the beach. Looking at the time, he noted the nearness they both were to the magic hour. "Well, will you look at that, five minutes to midnight. Nearly the witching hour," he remarked, softening his tone of voice. "Time enough, I suppose, for one last story."

"I'm listening," Anna replied, sitting back down in her chair.

Luke's grin held a hint of mischief. "Good, because this one is a doozy…"

**THE MAZE**

A blur, a memory of something. A boy, a beautiful little boy. With blonde hair, green eyes. He laughed through the mist as police sirens wailed out, followed by banging noises and two gun shots. And then, silence. Nothing. Just the vast emptiness.

Circular, round, a ball of light at the end of a deep, long tunnel. It was like viewing the top of a well from the depths below. Suddenly, swirling towards her, the glow hit with force, engulfing the place with brightness. Then a breath of life as a woman awoke, ruffling in some kind of packaging, with no memory of how or why she was there. Piercing a hole, she crawled out under a crimson sky, where crows cawed and circled above, a murder of them.

A lifeless woodland lay all around. Nothing seemed to grow in this nature reserve however, well, at least nothing good, merely decay and dankness. Maggots soiled the ground along with other wriggling infestations. Why was this woman inside a bin bag? How did she get there? There was a large, dead, black tree trunk and a cracked gravestone with the name 'Thomas' on it beside her.

The woman looked around, feeling dazed and confused. Scratching the back of her dark-haired scalp her head rang with something cruelly reminiscent that she couldn't quite put her finger on. "Where am I? Who am I?" How did I get here?" she asked herself, looking to her odd surroundings and then down at the dirt-ridden rags she was wearing, that appeared more like a prison inform than actual clothes.

Then, people came? Random people walked by, in dingy outerwear like her own. The strangers began whispering inaudible things but the woman held back, unsure of the situation. The whispers grew louder and louder, still sounding like gibberish, hurting the woman's ears, until she finally spoke: "Hello! Can you help me? I can't remember who I am?" The people merely continued to watch and murmur to each other. Her head rattling, the woman began to beg. "Do you know who I am? Please! I can't remember!" she shouted out, as she dragged her feet slowly towards them, making them to stop abruptly, their faces shrunken in on themselves as they then began to withdraw into the woods.

"Where are you going?"

Suddenly, a ruby red light roared through a crack in the bark of the tree trunk as disturbing noises begin to erupt. Smoke bled out from the tree along with two demonic hands that tore through the crack, opening it wider, revealing a monstrous looking Minotaur. It stomped forward with an aggressive growl. As the beast loomed over, drooling, sheer terror washed over the woman. Making her escape, she tripped over the grave beside her, soon bringing herself to her feet, she ran, fast, into the woods as scowling monstrous Greek eyes watched her, soon following.

Jumping over spikes, bushes, unearthed roots and deep pits in the ground the woman sped along, not daring to turn around, as she heard the galloping hooves close behind.

Then the woman saw something, something out of place. A road, and not just that, a service station, abandoned and derelict. And then a girl, a teenage girl, her hair like night rain, black and slick. She was hunched over rummaging through a grotty backpack, unaware of the amnesia struck woman hurtling towards her. She jumped on to the girl, clinging on for life, digging her nails deep into the girl's arm which rose, brandishing a knife. The woman shook, holding her hands up for mercy, still looking at her with fear.

"What the hell? Get off me!" the girl yelled, threatening to use her weapon on the woman.

"You have to help me! Please!" the woman implored, jerking her neck around. "Something is following me." She grabbed the girl's collar to look more closely at her face.

Then a terrifying roar trembled through the land. The girl's face melted from angered confusion to sudden panic. "Oh no, no, no." Her gaze widened, lowering her knife as she backed away.

"Do you know what it is?"

"Yeah, I do, and it's not good," the girl replied, picking up her bag. She looked around, and then to the service station, taking a step toward. The woman did too, not before being pushed back by the knife. "Back off, bitch. Don't follow me." The girl hissed.

Another roar bellowed out, causing the crows above to fly off in retreat. The two females twisted in fear as the girl leapt into the store. The woman somehow managed to sneak her way in behind, survival from the beast on her mind more than the strange girl who was no threat in comparison. Instantly, the girl grabbed a chair without even looking at it, as if she'd done this before and wedged it perfectly underneath the doorknob. It temporarily blocked it, at least, as they hid under the counter.

"You bitch!" The girl whispered with fury. "You damn selfish bitch, it was only after you! Now we're both dead." Her fist punched down to the floor.

"I'm sorry, I didn't know what else to do."

"And that's my problem how?"

Banging and grunts began to rumble the walls of the place as the two fugitives hid in fear.

"What is that thing?" the woman asked.

"Shut up!" the girl snapped. "I'm trying to think."

Feeling the sting of tears, her brain fried, the woman said, "I'm sorry, I don't know what's going on?" In her distress, she failed to notice the sudden silence. "I don't know who I am! What is this place…?"

The girl's finger rose. "Wait, shut up!"

They both sat still, realising the banging had ceased.

The woman's face dropped. "It's stopped."

"Exactly," the girl said, standing carefully to see for herself that the beast had left, leaving only a mess and broken glass everywhere.

The woman soon followed, hiding behind the till. "Maybe it got bored?"

"Or maybe it's playing with its food."

Gulping the woman leant back against the wall. "What are we going to do?"

"Wait."

"For what?"

"To be sure! Sit down!" the girl ordered. The woman obeyed, perching down in a nest of dust covered magazines and newspapers.

The scavenger girl knelt down, exhaling in relief, before saying, "You don't remember who you are?"

"No, I only woke up about five minutes ago in a bin bag?" She frowned. "Where am I? What is this place?" she questioned. Her throat felt dry and sore as she spoke.

"Oh boy," the teen laughed. "Well, here's the thing, I don't know."

"You don't know?"

"No. None of us do," the girl replied, leaning her head back. "We all just wake up here, no understanding why or who we are. There are loads of us. Don't know what the hell this place is or what that thing is."

"The horns, the head. It looks like that Greek monster thing," the woman said.

"What 'Greek monster thing'?"

"The...the Minotaur?" she replied. "Yeah, that's it, the Minotaur, who chases people in the maze?"

The girl's head lowered in exhaustion. "Yeah, that sums this place up, one giant chaotic maze," she said, rubbing her neck.

"Maybe there's a centre? A way out?"

The teen's face creased at the idea. "Ha! Trust me, there's no centre," she said. "It's dangerous. I've seen a lot of people die. It's a dog eat dog world here. You'll learn that, soon enough."

"How long have you been here?" the woman asked.

"About seven years."

"Oh my God."

"You don't really think about it, not when you're constantly running, fighting or scavenging to survive." The girl blinked slowly, recalling it all. "Time just seems to melt here." Her gaze focussed down towards one of the newspaper headlines, pulling back in disgust.

"Awful! Can you imagine such a thing?"

"What?" The woman lifted the newspaper revealing the headline. 'Five-year-old boy killed in horrific murder'. There was a picture of the child. The woman momentarily felt a trigger of pain burn through her, like fire.

"I mean who could ever kill a little kid? There are some sick twisted shits out there," the girl commented, flicking through the pages.

A blurry swirl stung the core of the woman. She could hear the little boy's laugh, as she looked at the photo of him. Blonde and happy.

"I-I think I know that boy," the woman commented. She felt in her pocket, pulling out a folded up photo, of him.

The girl frowned. "How'd you know him?"

"I-I think he was my son."

"Right?" sneered the girl.

The boy, she knew him, she loved him, she was sure of it. Abrupt bangs suddenly hit the station shop door as the two survivors huddled together, the woman hiding the photo in her pocket, clenching it tight in there. The girl held her large glimmering knife upward, ready.

"It's okay, it's me!" a masculine voice called out.

The teenager sighed, lowering the weapon, as she got up to open the door to a scruffy man wearing a beanie hat that allowed his grey, straw-like hair to poke out of. His face seemed familiar, amphibious looking in nature, she knew him too, from somewhere?

"Who? Who's that?" the woman questioned suspiciously.

"An old associate."

Once the door was open, he entered with a certain swagger about him.

"Bitch, this is Rat Shit," she said.

The man offered a hand to the woman. "Nice to meet you," he said in a raspy voice.

"I know you?" She retracted her hand.

The man's face crinkled. "Do you?"

The girl drifted past them both casually. "Ignore her; she's in a bad way."

"Great just what we need, more damaged goods," he huffed, leaving the store with the girl, as the woman traipsed behind. "I saw what happened. Kept watch, it's gone," he confirmed.

A hand rushed to the woman's chest. "Thank God."

"And I've managed to find a new haven, a safe place," he said, holding on to the straps of his back pack of supplies.

The woman's brain jumped ahead. "At the farm?"

"Yeah, how'd you know that?"

Pausing for a moment, she admitted. "I don't know? I just do."

"Jeez, looks like we've found our own Mystic Meg over here," he teased.

The girl gestured to the man that the woman was nuts. He sniggered. "Well, I guess if we're gonna make it before sunset we should leave now," he stated, hoisting his belt as he set off, turning his back to the woman. She still stood in thought at all the questions she had. "You coming?"

"Yes," she answered, hobbling along behind them.

"Come on then, we've got a long journey ahead."

And hopefully, we won't get killed on the way," the girl added, taking a gander around the woody setting they were walking towards.

Time passed, and the heat made the air stink. Musky and muggy. Flies buzzed around and the girl swatted them off. They had been traipsing through the woods for far too long a time. Without question, the woman had definitely seen the skeletons of more than just a dead forest, but bringing this obvious point up, she felt, at this stage would only provoke her already angsty companions who seemed to know what they were doing and, better than that, knew where they were going. The woman dragged behind, however, feeling drained. She was sapped of energy. Her ankles felt heavy, and her movement varied from numb to sluggish.

"We've been walking for hours! How much further?" she groaned.

The man grinned, side-eying her back. "Not much further now."

Her arms felt heavier with every step she took. Like boulders hefting her down. "Do you know anything about…this place?" the woman questioned, in need of an equal blend of distraction and answers.

"Me?" the man thumbed to himself. "Nothing more than what you've been told I'm guessing. We all turn up here, no clue why, how or who we are. Don't over think it, you won't find any answers. None of us do. We eventually figure, things just happen, what the hell!" He shrugged, adjusting his backpack.

"Great!"

"That thing you saw rarely shows his ugly head," he explained. "Other people are the real danger, not the monsters."

"Apart from that, though, it's a lovely place," the girl added sarcastically.

The man stopped. "Actually, here's a good spot."

"Good spot?" The teen frowned. "For what?"

"For this," the man said, whipping out a gun and pointing it at them both as they froze in surrender.

"God damn it!" the girl flared. "You really are a piece of shit aren't you."

The man nodded in response. "Yup."

"What the hell! How can you do this? How long have we known each other?"

"Long enough."

"Bastard."

"Sorry, it's just business. Now you're going to do exactly what I say, don't do anything stupid." He pointed the gun without compromise, a steely glint of determination in his gaze.

The girl swallowed hard, her life seemingly on the line, she looked behind him as he followed her eye movements. "Ah crap. He's here," she said as if the Minotaur were behind him.

"What?" the man responded, spinning round to see nothing, just as the girl attempted to run away. The man spun back round, starting to shoot, and missing with every wasted bullet. She made a quick escape, leaving the petrified woman behind, and alone.

"Bitch!" the man fired seeing the girl veer off as he grabbed the frantic woman by the scruff of her neck, dragging her down to knees. He pointed the gun at the back of her head as she cried, knowing this was most likely to be the end. She cowered down, away from him. The watchers from before began whispering once more.

"Please! Help!" she called out, with no response.

"Shut up! No one's gonna helping you," he grunted, pushing her hard to the ground as she wept. "Stay down! Flat!" he ordered, as she lay hysterical, like a snake ready to be beheaded. "I tell you being here as long as I have you begin to get more and more…bored. There's not much this wasteland can offer in terms of entertainment, well except for this." He lowered himself on top of her and began to caress her all over, licking her ear. A differing kind of crying now escaped the woman. "Oh come on now, am I not your type?" he chuckled, rising upward, jingling his loose belt. "Fair enough, lucky for you, that's not what I had in mind anyway. I was thinking of another source of entertainment for you. Question is, how should I do it?" He pulled out a line of weapons from his backpack, first a blade, then a hammer, and then a drill. The woman screamed at the man's obvious joy. "Oh I think we have a winner!"

Bending back down with the gun and drill both pointed at the woman's head she began to splutter and spit, begging for mercy. "Please, please!"

"I should tell you, this is really gonna hurt." He grinned as the drill began, inches away from her skull, ready to penetrate her skin. Then she heard a sudden whack. The drill stopped. The woman paused, then moved quickly aside as the man toppled over beside her, cradling his battered head. It was the girl, come back to save her, with a large stick in her hand with which she then proceeded to beat the man's head into oblivion as if it were a watermelon. Bruised and bloodied, he finally he stopped breathing. He lay dead, his head split open like a piñata, for all this wretched world to see.

Everything seemed to freeze to the woman at the sheer horror of it all. Her senses were suddenly heightened, she had never seen anyone die in front of her before, well at least, not that she could recall. Yet there was again another strange sense of familiarity to it all. She found herself painfully aware of everything around her. The smell of sweat mixed with flesh and bone, the steady slip of tears down her angular cheekbones and their salty flavour, the coppery taste of blood and fear on her tongue. Through the mists of shock the girl lurched over the corpse.

"Bullets are too good for you," she said, dropping the gooey stick and looking down at the lifeless body. She picked up his gun which was metres away amongst the leaves. The others, the spectators, huddled around the man's body and began devouring him like rabid animals, tearing out his organs and intestines, wearing them like party boas. The woman, disgusted by the sight, almost failed to realise the girl's hand being offered to her.

"Come on!" she yelled as the woman took the hand of her saviour, feeling a strong circulatory pulse suddenly as they turned to watch the swarm eat. "Vultures," the girl added, pushing the woman ahead before a roar bellowed out. The Minotaur had finally caught up to them. "Come on, let's get out of here," the teenage heroine insisted, running away, with her sidekick following.

"Where to?"

Looking quickly around, the girl pointed to a large church ahead, which seemed to appear out of nowhere. "Look! There! We can hide in there," she said, as they made their way hastily towards the monastery across a wasteland of crops, populated with living corpses, embedded as scarecrows that had crows feasting on their open organs. As they passed, they groaned, called and reached out to be helped, but the pair had problems of their own to deal with. Before long they managed to run to the outside of the church, with the beast following their trail but, for now, nowhere in sight.

"Think we're gonna be okay," the girl gasped, making her way towards the door of the church. The woman suddenly doubled over in burning agony as she heard the child's laughter once again. "What are you doing? Get up!" the girl barked.

The woman winced, sitting down on a nearby rock, recalling the child's face. "It's that kid, the one in the newspaper. I keep getting an image of him in flashbacks, but not flashbacks. It's more of a memory but something's blocking me from remembering." The girl peered at her, curious by the memory herself. "All I remember is his beautiful blonde hair and big green eyes, I took care of him." The woman nodded smiling, though not quite sure why, as a tear trickled down her cheek. "I can feel the love I have for him, but when I think of his face in my memories, he's just a blur. I loved him. But something obviously happened. I must have lost him or something. Because every time I think of him I just want to cry." Her head lowered in shame and the girl seemed to show a flicker of remorse toward her companion's distress.

Looking out to the open battlefield she lowered herself down and spoke urgently. "Enough of that talk. We have to be strong to survive. Yes?"

"Yes?"

"Good. Look we're here." Her hand signalled to the chained doors of the church as the Minotaur's roar echoed through the trees, causing the crows to erupt outward and head over to circle them high in the blood red sky.

"Quickly, let's sneak in round the back, it will be open," the girl said hurriedly, grabbing the woman's arm as they circled round the church.

*Wait, how does she know the back door is open?* the woman pondered, but let it pass. The girl struggled to twist the handle but, eventually, it turned. Entering into pitch black, if felt like the woman's worst nightmare, as the door creaked shut behind them, their fate felt sealed. It was cold. Glass crunched beneath their feet as they crept forward.

"It's pitch black in here! I can't see a damn thing!" the woman said.

The girl huffed. "Quit moaning. Be useful."

"How?"

"Feel for a switch or something," she said. "Actually, wait a sec, think I've found one." A wiggling metallic movement began.

"Thank God, I've always been scared of the dark," the woman admitted, with no idea how she knew this.

A burst of light flooded the room, revealing indeed a church, but one of twisted intent and devotion. One that housed, what appeared to be, a television show. There were screens and cameras everywhere. The woman's every reaction was being recorded, enlarged above and yet again below. The satanic stained glass displayed foreboding symbols, images and fiery lighting. A stage full of the watchers she had bumped into all day laughed at her.

The girl grinned sadistically to the sides, leaning on a clearly labelled light switch as two strangers grabbed the woman and bound her to a chair centre stage. Then, from the shadows, the man with the beanie hat, who seemingly had died in the woods, only moments ago, emerged in a suit, holding a microphone and waving to his audience.

"What the…"

"Thank you! Thank you!" The man bellowed, his rough accent now replaced by a more refined tone.

Both the man and the girl walked in front of the crowd of people and bowed, taking in their applause with honour.

The woman was beyond confused. "Wait! What's going on? What is this? Some kind of sick, twisted prank show?" she asked as the pair turned to her, all tied up still.

"Ha! No, I'm afraid not," he replied.

"Then what?" She frowned, the colour draining from her face. "What is this place?"

"Congratulations, Miss Mary Elizabeth Saunders, on getting through your three point five millionth day away from the world of the living. And as punishment for your crimes of murder, kidnapping, lying, stealing and overall being a good for nothing bitch, you are here to spend your eternity in our home. Welcome to hell." His voice deepened, looking up to his master's image in the stained glass above.

The reality of the situation didn't quite hit Mary. "Hell?" she said, trying not to snigger, unconvinced. "Wait my crimes? What crimes?" she questioned, now in a fluster, as she shuddered deeply.

"Oh, that's right, it's always new to you at this point," he added, beginning to pace about. "Well, that's why we have my favourite portion of tonight's celebrations, the 'This is Your Life' moment." He moved across the stage to indicate a PowerPoint labelled 'Mary Saunders', with a photo of her which seemed to have been taken off of a social media platform.

"You, Mary Saunders, were a thirty-five-year-old, childless Greek historian who, on a sunny day, 5th September, decided to kidnap your neighbour's son, Thomas Dolden." Clicking a button, the slide revealed the beautiful blonde haired boy. "For six months you kept him in your cellar, caring for him, feeding him, 'loving him', until the police came knocking, that was when you decided to take the easy way out, wasn't it?" He paused momentarily for effect. "That was fine, taking your own miserable existence out of the picture, but taking poor Thomas with you because you couldn't bear to let anyone else have him, because you were convinced his parents had been mistreating him when in fact they hadn't, was another matter. Disgusting! You, lady, are truly disgusting. And hiding his body in a bin bag. I mean, you really are a piece of crap aren't you."

It all came back to Mary in that moment, the flare of the memory burst and burnt her senses, but she knew his parents had been mistreating him, or at least, it had seemed that way at the time. She was only trying to protect him from them, from the world, the world that had been so cruel to her. It was a kindness, well, that's what she had thought in the moment. But maybe, maybe it was wrong of her she realised; it wasn't her life to meddle with. Sobbing with regret at what she had done, the crowd began hurtling insults at her. "Murderer!"

"Oh, don't start crying," the man said. "I hate it when you start crying! I mean were there tears when you killed little Thomas, huh? Well, how do you like it now?"

"Please stop," she whimpered.

"Now do you understand? Hell doesn't change us, not any of us, it merely shows us who we really are."

"Karma's a bitch, and we are your karma," the girl said, as a matter of fact.

Mary began weeping, her heart completely broken. "Please, just kill me." Her cries and sorrow made the man smile, as he savoured it.

"Well, you're kind of already dead but I get your point," he joked. "And I'm sorry to say, there is no peace for you, not ever. It is your soul's purpose to now and forever relive this never-ending nightmare." His arms rose in a priest-like gesture as his voice echoed through one of hell's churches. Leaning into her, he stated, "No one gets away with sin. In the end everybody pays, everyone suffers."

The cameras zoomed in on Mary's face as she let out her despair. The audience revelled in the pain they witnessed, the torture.

The man's chin rose high with pride. "Get her out of here."

Two strangers undid her bounds and began slowly dragging her fragile frame away as the crowd threw more insults her way. Dead to the world, and this one too, she felt like a hollow shell. Her soul felt like butter that had, by this point, been spread across too thinly on a large and extremely dry piece of toast. Soon enough, the man, the girl and the crowd followed her to where she began, where she always began. By the tree trunk, cracked grave stone marked 'Thomas' and the open bin bag. The sky remained a garnet glow as the people began to leave, off into the woods. The murder of crows above circled and observed the proceedings below.

The man stood before her. "Any final words, for today I mean?"

"Kill me, please. Just end me."

"Ah, we've been through this…"

"But I'm not that person any more. I don't have those memories once you get rid of them."

"Yeah, but you remember eventually, you always do."

"Please," she begged.

He leant in. "Sorry, we don't make the rules."

"Come on big guy! You're up," the girl said, summoning the Minotaur from behind them. He growled at Mary as the girl knelt down to whisper in her ear. "You know every day we do this and, you always, one way or another, start talking about your Minotaur friend over there and how, in Greek mythology, r he chases people in mazes or something. At this point I always have to tell you that this is your maze, and here there is no centre it. There is no escape. Just eternity. Think of it as a game with no end, just...endless restarts." She sniggered. "Face it, you're nothing but a selfish, cowardly, nobody that no one cares about or ever did."

Mary's tears suddenly ceased and her eyes began to bulge. She turned her veiny neck to face the girl and man, hastening a frosty silence. "And who are you to judge me, huh? You're both here, so you must have done bad things. And you're not even the stars of your own hell, you're just nameless supporting characters in my eternal, never-ending suffering."

The girl paused, considering a response in her head before explaining with simmering restraint, "You are our suffering, having to deal with you forever is our hell." She paused as her words stung with blistering precision. "Sleep well, Mary, we've got a big day tomorrow. After all, we wouldn't want you to miss anything." Her hand tapped the top of Mary's dark head of hair as she wandered away, to take her place ready for the next round.

"If it helps, you won't remember a thing," the man sneered as he signalled the Minotaur, who came closer and closer.

"Please!" Mary cried out. "Please! No!"

The Minotaur then lifted his hairy hand and touched Mary's screaming face, causing her to fall asleep. Silent. The only bliss she would ever know before it would always begin again. Then...

A blur, a memory of something. A boy, a beautiful little boy. With blonde hair, green eyes. He laughed through the mist as police sirens wailed out, followed by banging noises and two gun shots. And then, silence. Nothing. Just the vast emptiness.

Circular, round, a ball of light at the end of a deep, long tunnel. It was like viewing the top of a well from the depths below. Suddenly, swirling towards her, the glow hit with force, engulfing the place with brightness. Then a breath of life as a woman awoke, ruffling in some kind of packaging, with no memory of how or why she was there. Piercing a hole, she crawled out under a crimson sky, where crows cawed and circled above, a murder of them.

A lifeless woodland lay all around. Nothing seemed to grow in this nature reserve however, well, at least nothing good, merely decay and dankness. Maggots soiled the ground along with other wriggling infestations. Why was this woman inside a bin bag? How did she get there? There was a large, dead, black tree trunk and a cracked gravestone with the name 'Thomas' on it beside her.

The woman gazed around dazed and confused, scratching the back of her dark-haired scalp as her head rang with something cruelly reminiscent she couldn't quite put her finger on. "Where am I? Who am I?" she asked, unaware that the nightmare had only just begun, all over again...

## CHAPTER SEVEN

"No rest for the wicked, forever and ever it would seem," Luke mused, his expression blank, his eyes dilated at the thought of his own words. The fire crackled beside him.

Anna almost choked in amusement. "Now, that, that was a good one." she admitted, clapping her hands together. "So...twisted."

"Thank you," Luke responded with a degree of pride, bowing his head. "I thought it up myself," he grinned.

"Yeah, it certainly had a satanic zing. I loved the twist. Got to say, I didn't see it coming."

"Well, all the clues were there, if you knew where to look," Luke said smoothly. "The soul is always just one minute short of judgement."

Fingers began to tighten on the dagger Anna had concealed beneath her. She composed herself before speaking. "Tell me something, Luke, do you think hell is real?"

"Oh, most definitely," he responded without thought.

"Really?"

"Oh, yes."

"How come?" Anna's face widened, so that she resembled a curious child.

"I just, have a feeling." The boy smiled, blending his own brand of charm and cheek which, in truth, Anna couldn't help but be attracted too. This new, confident psychosexual intensity caused a tingle in Anna. She had always found herself drawn to the intense, to intensity in general, like a fly to rotting flesh. Loosening her grip on the knife, yet still holding it, she hinted at a smirk as she listened to what more he had to say.

"I find the concept of sin pretty pointless now though, especially in the type of world we live in, the world is practically hell nowadays, so dark and cruel. No point in rules, not any more. Chaos has won, clearly. Why fight it?" Luke said.

Pondering on the thought, Anna spoke instinctively in response, as her throat began to dry. "Hmm…I suppose you have a point."

A glacial chill drifted over Luke's demeanour, suddenly taking hold as he cracked yet another devious smile. His eyes darted to glance at the clock. "Well…it's getting late, best get some shut eye," he said, rising tall as he politely offered Anna a hand.

Anna hesitated, resisting the urge to grunt before slipping her weapon deep within her sleeve, taking his cool palm and standing to meet him. "Yes," she agreed.

Letting the moment reside for a brief second, Luke then broke away and walked to the other side of the room, his finger dusting a nearby shelf. He paused and turned to speak to Anna. "We can phone for a taxi in the morning when, hopefully, my family show up. In the meantime, can I offer you my sister's room?" He gestured to the door just behind him.

Tempted but not stupid, Anna knew better than to be anywhere that wasn't close enough to the front door to make a quick escape with the stuff she had stolen, especially in a cabin with such creaky floorboards. "No, I'm good here thanks." She pointed to the leather sofa they had neglected to sit on all evening.

"Okay…" Luke's face twitched in response to the odd choice and then glanced around, grasping the nearest blanket he could see and passing it to her as a bed cover. "Here's a blanket. Feel free to make yourself at home, pull up the chairs, whatever you want to make yourself comfortable." He gestured around the room.

"Okay, thanks," she replied, as she started to ready her makeshift bed for the night. She lay down and heard the long drawn out squeak of the furniture as she covered herself and rested her weary head on a fuzzy fur cushion. She tucked herself in to make it seem like she intended to stay till morning.

"Are you sure there isn't anything I can get you?" Luke said kindly. His big blue twinkled under heavy lashes.

"No. I'm good, thanks," Anna replied, snuggling herself in-between the raunchy leather and the itchy, ill-patterned cover that was frayed at the ends. Luke was clearly sold on her actually staying. Anna sighed and felt the cool slice of her knife graze up against her wrist.

"Okay, goodnight then," Luke said, turning the light off with a simple flick. The only light now came from the blue glow of the full moon through the windows and the apocalyptic fire that raged on through the night. The rain splattered and the wind roared against the wooden structure of the cabin.

Luke lingered at the door, in the moonlight, a playful smile on his lips. Anna waved to him as an indication that it was time to leave. "Goodnight," she said.

"Sweet dreams," he whispered across the room.

"You too."

"Shout if you need anything," he said, turning around to be engulfed by the darkness of the hallway to his room.

"Will do," she called out to him, listening to his footsteps until finally her ears heard the door of his room shut. She then slipped one foot out from under the blanket, down to the floorboards, then another, as she tossed the bedding all together to one side. She trod carefully, to avoid any chance of creaking floorboards giving her away. She walked over to the long hallway and peered down into the gloom to confirm that Luke had gone to bed. The door was shut. The scavenger girl sighed in relief, dropping her nice girl act and whispering to herself, "Thank God. The fucker just doesn't shut up."

She began carefully sneaking about, stealing some odd bits and pieces that looked vaguely expensive, filling her pockets, even grabbing Luke's car keys. She wanted to be out of there sooner rather than later, before Luke's family finally decided to make their entrance. More casualties she wouldn't want to befriend. More blood on her hands.

Pulling out her sharpened blade, Anna looked at her reflection in a nearby mirror, a silver glimmer from the knife scared across her regretful face. *Don't look at me like that,* she thought. She had to do this. She had to kill Luke, no matter how much of a nice guy he seemed. No matter. He was a witness to her, he had seen her face, could remember it. But not her name; not her real name. She had made sure of that. He had to go though, he knew too much. He could easily tell on her, but would he? "No," she told herself, purging the idea of sentiment and mercy from her brain, clasping the handle of her knife. "I have to do this. I have to survive. I don't want to but…I have to." She turned to see a handsomely charming picture of Luke on a shelf, gazing at her, melting her Arctic heart of ice.

He may receive the privilege of a shed tear after all this, just the one, but not for his death, no, this 'Anna' learnt long ago not to waste tears on the dead, but she would, perhaps, manage a drop of sadness for the kindness he had shown her, the light he brought into the world that she would soon extinguish. Nevertheless, it had to be done. Letting one go never ended well. She'd made that mistake before, and it always came back to bite her. Letting one go, every now and again, a little victim spared because they reminded her of someone else, because they had freckles, because they were a child. And that's how she lived with herself. That's how she kept doing the awful things that she kept doing. Because once, in a while, if the mood was right, she happened to be kind. It was a fool's error. Not one she intended to make again.

Perhaps she could return the kindness he had shown all night and make it quick? A swift flick of her wrist, slicing his throat open? Yes that would do it. Taking a step further, something compelled her to pull back, back to the photo. His face. How could she? Her mind was telling her do kill him but the rest of her just couldn't.

And then, she felt something she hadn't felt in some time. She was ashamed of her quivering weakness. This stupid boy had somehow touched her soul with his kindness, something she also hadn't seen for a while. 'Anna' had been alone for so long, it was a relief to her that she had, in a way, found an equal, someone who didn't seem to judge. Even if that person, at first, had come in the initial guise of prey, he was a fun pet, one she had doubts about snuffing out of this world. One she knew now, she couldn't snuff out. And, unlike the other characters in her stories she had been weaving all night, 'Anna' had tonight decided to maybe, just maybe, let Luke go.

She had what she needed anyway. And Luke was a rare breed; decent enough to live. She smiled, turning back to her reflection as she spruced her locks up. *Let him go. Take what you can, don't turn around, run and just keep going. Yes,* she concluded, putting her knife away. She continued her search for things she could sell for good cash. Rummaging through odds and sods, scraps until finally circling her way around the room to Chuckles the doll whose head she gleefully snapped off and threw to one side. She then picked up the Haiti Hoodoo statue, cradling and fingering it in the palm of her hand. She eyed it up and down with a condescending gaze and giggled.

"Cursed? We'll see about that," she whispered. "I wish to finally get the one thing I've always wanted, what I have always deserved, some damn peace from stupid mumbo jumbo shit!" Her voice filled with venom as she threw the doll down, snapping it's fragile frame in half as she stepped over its broken form.

Pocketing some antiques, her magpie eye was then drawn to a crystal encrusted nouveau style box. He nails clacked against the clasp as she fiddled with the lid. Suddenly, ungodly an howl called out as lighting flashed across the sky with a roar of thunder. Petrified, 'Anna' dropped the box and brought herself too, unveiling her knife from her sleeve. She clutched at her beating heart. That wasn't like anything she had ever heard before. "Hello?" she called out, not knowing where the noise had come from until another painful shrill beaconed from a door, a door housed in the kitchen. The cellar.

Swallowing her instinct to just leave, 'Anna' decided she would investigate whoever or whatever it was down there. It was clearly distraught and in need of help. Whether it was her newfound sense of morality or not, coupled by the general intrigue, 'Anna' just couldn't pull herself away. She approached cautiously, keen to discover what lurked below. With every step she took, the lightning lit the way.

"Hello? Is there someone there?" she asked, sweating heavily.

An unearthly scream echoed again. *How was Luke not hearing this?* she wondered as she lifted her knife, turning the doorknob ready for anything. Swinging the door open she saw only steps trailing down into silent darkness before her. Then, as another bolt lit, a further scream whelped out, illuminated vaguely by the glow. A mangled, stitched together, assortment of beings tried to claw its way up the stairs towards her. A thing with arms, three…four arms, and one leg. It looked deformed with its pustulous skin, and wisps of frail dead hair. Its bloodshot, demon eyes seemed to cry, as the light caught it, and thick, glooping snot dribbled directly into the monster's open wet mouth as it shrieked.

"Oh my God!" 'Anna' gasped, lowering her knife. "What the hell!" she said, as another bang, crash and flash crossed the sky. She was unaware that a tall figure had crept up behind her, as the being below bellowed in fear of the approaching shadow. Turning round too late, 'Anna' felt the brutal knock of something hit the back of her head and, before she could even feel it, she was out cold. Unconscious. Fast asleep.

A crackling noise brought 'Anna' round. Her head rung. It was a familiar noise, one of logs burning. An amber glow formed as she slowly opened her eyes, wriggling a little to feel that she was bound. Her vision blurred, she looked down. She was tied to a chair, the one she had been sat in all night. Exhaling, she felt the air restricted. Her mouth was gagged, and tightly, with some kind of cloth. Her vision now focusing better she gazed across to her captor. It was Luke, in his chair, leaning back with a certain confidence he had been holding back all night. His shirt had popped open to reveal his chest and his glasses were now gone. He was shrouded in darkness, omitting an oppressive energy that felt soul sucking, a hot steaming miasma of beautiful black nothing that rippled off his now menacing aura. He was swirling a glass of whisky in one hand as his other felt the warmth of the flames beside them, before noticing that 'Anna' was stirring.

"Oh, you're awake, finally. I was beginning to get worried," he wickedly lied, looking down at her.

Overcome with emotion, 'Anna' began to wriggle but to no avail. Luke watched on, his jaw tensing in sadistic pleasure at her struggle and failed attempt to free herself.

"Don't bother." He signalled with his hand. "Let's not waste any time and make this quick, shall we? I guess you're wondering what that thing is in the basement. Any guesses?"

'Anna' murmured, nearly choking on the cloth gagging her. Luke furrowed his brow and his finger rushed to his ear, signalling for her to speak up. "Huh? I'm sorry I can't hear you, that gag makes it impossible doesn't it." He bit his lip. "Here let me help you," he said, pulling off the restraint as she glared hotly at him.

"Listen…" she hissed. "I don't know and I don't care, just let me go." Her tone was scornful, before soon shifting to that of fear. "Please. I won't tell anyone what I saw. Please, just let me go."

Rolling his eyes in displeasure, Luke bellowed. "Wrong! Let us make a deduction. Tell me, what did you see?" he questioned as if some kind of mentor, teaching his apprentice.

"A-a thing." 'Anna' hesitated. "It looked human but not human."

"Much like your wolf in the woods tonight that apparently chased you, but we both know didn't actually happen." He leant in. "So tell me what did you see?"

"A thing. A thing with arms, three or four arms, and one leg. It looked deformed." Her voice whimpered slightly in recollection.

"Good. And what else?"

"It looked like a girl."

"Bingo. Any guesses who that was?"

"Listen I don't know."

"Anna!"

"Oh! Your sister?" Anna guessed, simply due to the wisps of blonde hair. She had noticed in the family photo before that everyone was brunette except for her and Luke.

"Correct!" he confirmed.

'Anna' was repulsed. The girl was unrecognisable and so young. "Why?" she asked.

"Why? Why does one pop a balloon? Or burn a city down? Because I got bored." He shrugged unapologetically. "So like the doctor in your baby monster story, I created something new." His hands gestured theatrically. "Don't worry, she's asleep now. For good this time."

Taking a moment to evaluate the situation, 'Anna' breathed evenly. She had faced dangerous men before, but nothing quite like him. "Where are the rest of your family then? Your younger brothers, your parents?"

Luke froze momentarily, then giggled naughtily. He soon proceeded to cackle uproariously. Anna didn't get the joke. "What's so funny?" she questioned as he halted his laughing fit to respond.

"You thought they tasted the same."

Anna sat utterly perplexed and then the room spun as the realisation hit. "No!" The scavenger girl gulped. The food earlier, the beef. "It was, it was…"

"But mother…" Luke said with a savouring look as he licked his lips with his tongue, "was definitely more tender in my opinion."

Anna looked sickened, the colour draining from her face, as she began to gag realising what she had consumed. Disgust hit her system like a train at full pelt.

Luke sprang up as if on a stage. "You see everything, every tale tonight, every one we have discussed and told has happened in one form or another. Exactly as I planned, but well, you know, I never do get the credit I truly deserve do I?" he mused, before continuing. "The best and worst things happen in the wings don't they, back stage, in the shadows. I guess you have figured by now that this is all a very long winded way of me of telling you that…you should never judge a book by its cover. Should you?" he asked, lowering down to adjust her top.

"Go to hell!" she hissed through gritted teeth.

"Oh, I've been, thank you, it's quite the tourist attraction," he joked, with a sigh of disappointment. "You know, I had such high hopes for you. Miss Stephanie Russo."

The hair on her arms stood on end as he said that, she couldn't hide her guilty look. "How do you…?"

"How do I know your real name?" he replied, finishing her sentence with a chuckle. "I know everything." Luke finished his drink before slamming the empty glass down on a table. "Who you are, all the things you've done, your sins. I had such high hopes for you, but you had to go soft in the end didn't you! I hate it when they get all soft," he said out loud to himself, leaning against the mantle.

"What are you talking about?" The girl scrunched up her face. "What was this some kind of test?"

"In a way, one you failed."

"I…I don't understand."

"No, and I'm sorry to say you probably never will. You see, if the stories tonight have proven anything it's that times are changing. The world is changing. It is changing into a world I have been working tirelessly to bring forth. A world without the hypocrisy of rules, a world inhabited by the types of people that won't just eat the forbidden fruit but cut down the whole damn tree," Luke growled in her face, before breaking into a grin and turning away.

"You know, I have always believed that all people, when narrowed down to their core, are just evil little fuckers," he continued. "Now, I'm sure you're wondering how this affects you? Well it doesn't. For a time, tonight, I thought maybe you could be part of my new world. But I'm sorry, no. Just no."

"You're crazy," she said, beginning to wilt from heat and fear.

"And I thought I was just a little eccentric. But I take your point."

"Who the hell are you? Really?"

Luke smirked. "Who am I? Why, my dear, have you not figured it out yet?" He paused, before adding, "Well, I'm sure as hell not Luke Foster, though I do enjoy inhabiting his hulk of a body." He grinned theatrically, feeling his own muscles. "I'm the daddy of demons, the king of chaos, the dawn of doom. The fallen angel that saved humanity from blissful ignorance with truthful knowledge. I have many titles. I am HIM, dear girl, the one and only. In the flesh. Here, with you." His lip curled in what could be interpreted as a sneer, or a snarl.

"And wha-what do you want?"

"What do I want?" he mimicked, resting his claw-like fingers on her wrists as he leant over like a vulture. "Well, that's simple…to save you all, all over again. You see…I'm here to give this wretched world the ending it deserves…" His voice became demonic, developing into an animalistic growl. Seconds later a hellish roar bellowed out of the angelic looking boy as fangs hurled their way toward 'Anna's' screaming face, sinking their way into her flesh as blood squirted from every direction. A red river cascaded down the remnants of what was left of face, as if now hanging by a thread. She now tasted her own blood, welling up inside her own drowning throat. The last thing Stephanie Russo, also known as 'Anna', would ever wish, hope even, is that this hell would soon be over…

No one escapes from life alive 'Luke' noted to himself. His shirt was wide open as outside the winds of change blew harder than ever before. The beast cracked his neck like a glow stick, letting out a grunt of relief. He was sitting now, picking bits of the lifeless girl from his teeth. Her remains lay on the floor wrapped in the rug, disrespectfully acting as a foot rest beneath his hefty heels.

Soon he began wiping the last remnants of blood from his chin. *That parasite of a girl tasted like black liquorice*, so moorish. He sucked his fingers, not wanting to waste a single drop. Exquisite. He had played that amusement of a femme fatale like a violin and cut her strings, the thought of that alone tickled his mammoth sized ego.

Swirling yet another glass of the whisky that paired up so well with his meal, this king moved a hand towards the fire. Its ruthless wrath reminded him of his pit. Was he feeling homesick? No. Never! A new kingdom needed to be formed; a tenth circle. Soon this world would be remade in his image and the last remnants of good would die. It was all part of the plan. Yes, he knew, everything was about to change. Another sip of whisky washed down his throat nicely. It burned as good as the dream he had fantasised repeatedly in his head. With a click of his taloned fingers, the radio began to play 'I Don't Want to Set the World on Fire'. 'Luke' grinned, looking deep into the fire as, outside, the storm roared on. He sipped his drink contentedly, repeating over and over to himself, "And so it begins, and so it begins…"

And lest we forget, the devil works miracles too.

Copyright © George Morris De'Ath, 2020

Printed in Great Britain
by Amazon